THE CLUE OF THE MARKED CLAW

KEN HOLT *Mystery Stories*

"We pick up its location with the radio direction finder,"
Jackson said. "You know the rest."

The Clue of the Marked Claw

THE CLUE OF THE MARKED CLAW

By Bruce Campbell

GROSSET & DUNLAP *Publishers*

NEW YORK

PRINTED IN THE UNITED STATES OF AMERICA

CONTENTS

CONTENTS

THE CLUE OF THE MARKED CLAW

CHAPTER I

PEACE AND QUIET!

THE BLUE ATLANTIC spread out before them as far as the boys could see, its ripples catching the sun and throwing up dazzling points of light. Directly below them, small waves moved up the beach and then retreated again, and far out a smudge of smoke signaled the passing of a distant ship.

"Nothing like the ocean, is there?" It was the red-headed young giant who spoke. His sport shirt was stretched taut by the spread of his shoulders, and his flaming hair towered half a head above his companion, leaning beside him against the door of the red convertible. "What's the matter?" Sandy Allen added a moment later. "Nothing to say?" His freckled face broke into a grin. "For you that's something of a record."

Sandy's lean, dark-haired partner in so many adventures stirred, and his bright eyes swung away from the water. "I was thinking—a process you wouldn't know about."

"Not that!" Sandy drew back in mock alarm. "Every time you start thinking we get into trouble."

1

Ken Holt spoke quietly. "I was thinking of the time you and I got our first look at Skeleton Island."

The grin left Sandy's face. "That wasn't so funny," he said.

Ken's thoughts raced over the events that later became known as "The Secret of Skeleton Island." He recalled how he had set forth alone to rescue his father, the famous foreign correspondent, Richard Holt, from a desperate situation—and how helpless he would have been if the Allen family hadn't stepped in to lend a hand.

But that was all past now—or the danger, at least, was past. What remained was the good part of that adventure—the fact that the Allen clan had practically adopted him, and given him the first real home he had known since his mother's death years before. Richard Holt, who was almost always off in some strange corner of the world, gathering the exclusive news that made him the ace reporter of the Global News Service, was as pleased over the new arrangement as Ken himself was, and as devoted to Ken's new family: Sandy himself, Pop Allen, Sandy's older brother Bert, and tiny Mom Allen, who ran her huge husband and her two huge sons as surely as they ran the weekly Brentwood *Advance*.

"It wasn't all bad—that mess," Ken said. "After all, I met you and your—"

"Cut it out!" There weren't many things that Sandy was afraid of, but praise was one of them.

"O.K." It was Ken's turn to grin. "I won't say another word. I won't even mention the way you ran like a scared rabbit to avoid Mrs. Brown's thanks a couple of days ago."

"You didn't exactly wait around for them yourself," Sandy retorted. "But I thought we'd agreed not to talk about—what was it we decided to call it?—'The Black Thumb Mystery.' Let's get going, huh?" He got back into the car.

"Check." Ken had no more desire to think about their recent adventure than Sandy had. In fact, it was he who had suggested that they both accept a long-standing invitation from one of Ken's former schoolmates to spend a week out on the tip of Long Island, where they would have nothing on their minds but sun and sand and sea.

Ken slid under the wheel and guided the car back onto the road. "Only about twenty miles to go," he said.

Sandy wriggled until his broad back made a comfortable dent in the red leather upholstery. "Tell me about the Batesons." He glanced sideways at Ken. "Maybe I shouldn't have come along—they don't know me."

"Don't be a chump. Any invitation I get automatically includes you." Ken tapped the horn and eased around a slow farm truck. "I've already told you most of what I know about the Batesons. I think you'll like Ted. He's shorter than I am, but his shoulders are nearly as big as yours. He played center for two years. I don't know his family. They've been out here in Eastend for generations, and always owned some fishing boats. Ted wrote that now they do a lot of lobstering during the summer and fall."

"Lobsters," Sandy murmured approvingly. "That's for me."

"And peace and quiet."

"Naturally. You have to have peace and quiet to enjoy a broiled lobster. Though I wouldn't mind going out on the boat once, if they'd take us."

"They probably will take us along on one of their trips. And Ted says there's good fishing and a swell beach."

Sandy sighed. "Sounds perfect to me."

Five miles went by in relaxed silence, and then Sandy roused himself to open the glove compartment in the dashboard. He rummaged around for a moment, spilling an accumulation of road maps, small tools, and rags out onto the floor.

Then he looked at Ken accusingly. "Didn't we have a bar of chocolate in here?"

"You ate it an hour ago."

"We had a spare."

"That's the one you ate two hours ago." Ken fished around in his jacket pocket. "Here." He handed over half a bar. "I saved this—knew you'd be needing emergency rations."

"What's in the envelope?"

Ken glanced down and saw that he had pulled an envelope out of his pocket along with the chocolate. "Oh! I'd forgotten all about it. It's from Global—came this morning just as we were leaving. I was going to read it on the way. Open it up."

"O.K. It's from Granger," Sandy added a moment later, spreading out the sheet. "And there's a check attached!" He whistled. "One hundred bucks!"

"Just in time," Ken said. "Our treasury was about bankrupt. What's Granger got to say?"

Sandy swallowed a mouthful of chocolate and cleared his throat. " 'Dear Ken and Sandy: Am enclosing a check for the pix and the background material for the Black Thumb yarn. I suppose you know we scooped them all on that story, thanks to you two. A cable from your father today, Ken, says he's flying straight from Mexico to Peru, on some lead he's picked up. Also says to tell you to keep out of trouble for a change and to have a good time lobstering. I echo these sentiments—but suggest you keep your eyes peeled nevertheless. You never can tell where a story'll break, but they seem to break around your heads with startling regularity. Yours for bigger and better lobsters and bigger and better scoops. . . .' "

Sandy stuffed the letter back into its envelope. "Some sense of humor Granger's got. He doesn't care what happens to us, so long as he gets the story first. I prefer your father's less selfish attitude."

Ken tried to conceal a grin. He knew that the pictures Sandy had sold to Global News were the greatest triumphs of his life. "Here's where we leave the ocean and head for the bay," he said, slowing the car to turn left off the highway.

A moment later they had their first glimpse of the quieter "inside" water, and not long after that they were entering a tiny village built around the half-mile-across harbor. A narrow inlet opened into the big bay beyond, and a stone tower on one side of the cut supported a light that could be seen even in daylight, blinking monotonously on and off.

The road they were on ended at a building whose far wall, supported on wooden piles, extended over the water. A weather-beaten sign identified the structure as the Eastend Wholesale Fish Company.

Ken stopped the car. "I'll ask for the Batesons' house," he said, crawling out. When he returned, a moment later, he said, "We take the lane on the right. It's the last house."

They drove slowly along the road skirting the bay, past comfortable houses with grassy lawns and gardens. Each property on the water side of the road had its own pier, extending out into the harbor like a spoke from the rim of a wheel.

When they passed a mailbox bearing the name PAUL ANTHONY Ken eased up on the accelerator. "It's the next house."

Several hundred feet beyond the mailbox he pulled into a driveway and stopped alongside a large wooden house, gleaming with a new coat of white paint. From where they sat they could see that the driveway went on past a shed and stopped at a sturdy-looking pier extending some seventy-five feet into the water.

They had scarcely opened the doors of the car when the front door of the house swung wide, and a middle-aged woman came out on the porch hastily wiping her hands on her apron. Her hair was graying, but her walk and brisk manner were youthful. She smiled as she came down the three shallow steps.

"You must be Ken and Sandy," she said, holding out a hand to each. "I'm Mary Bateson—Ted's mother. Welcome to Eastend."

The smile on her face was even warmer than the

words. "Come along in. Ted's out with one boat, and my husband's out with the other," she explained, as she led the way, "but they'll be home in an hour or so. You'll just have time to get settled and learn your way around."

The boys approved the way she left them alone the minute she had showed them to their room, and when they had put down their bags they moved with one accord toward the windows overlooking the harbor. Directly north of them the inlet marker light blinked on and off—more visible now as the sun sank lower. From the windows facing westward they could look back to the main corner of the little village, dominated by the wholesale fish company's building. The adjoining house—the one whose mailbox had indicated that it belonged to PAUL ANTHONY—had a shed and a pier similar to that on the Bateson property.

"Pretty nice," Sandy said finally, backing away to fall on one of the two beds, and bounce up and down to test its softness.

Ken sniffed appreciatively at the salt air. "Shouldn't have any trouble sleeping here."

"When did you ever have trouble getting to sleep?" Sandy snorted. "Staying awake is your problem."

"Come on down when you're finished," Mrs. Bateson's voice floated up to them a few minutes later as they were opening their bags. "I've fixed up a couple of sandwiches. We won't be eating supper for two hours yet."

Sandy grinned. "Ah! That's what I call a thoughtful hostess."

Half an hour later they were assuring her that they had eaten all they could hold, and that she mustn't take time out from her household duties to entertain them.

"There's a rowboat at the pier," she said. "Or maybe you'd like to try your hand at crabbing? You'll find the nets in the shed."

"Don't worry about us," Ken told her. "We can keep busy just loafing."

"Good." She smiled. "I knew when I saw you that you were the kind of guests we like."

With a leisurely air the boys wandered out the back door and down the driveway. Sandy poked his head into the open shed, pointing out to Ken the endless yards of fish nets hanging from the rafters, the outboard motor on its rack in one corner, and the two rowboats turned upside down in another. A small truck and a sedan stood side by side just inside the entrance.

The water murmuring gently beneath the pier was so clear that they could see its sandy bottom some ten feet below. Small fish darted between the pilings and a large crab scuttled across their field of view.

"Want to go crabbing?" Sandy pointed to the rowboat tied to the pier.

"I don't seem to want to do much of anything." Ken stifled a yawn.

Sandy grinned, but an instant later he yawned too. "It's so quiet here," he said defensively, and then he added, "There's a nice patch of grass beyond the shed."

Without further pretense of energy they made their way to it and settled down with their backs against the silvered shingles of the shed wall.

"We'll hear the boats when they come in," Ken said.

"Oh, sure."

The sun was warm and the leaves of the fruit trees surrounding the house whispered drowsily.

"This is my idea of a vacation," Sandy mumbled, after another prodigious yawn.

Ken scarcely heard him. His eyes were already closed.

In the distance a sea gull shrieked faintly, and then there was silence.

Some time later—Ken had no idea how long he had been asleep—he suddenly jerked into consciousness, aroused by the sounds directly behind him. In another moment he had oriented himself—remembered where he was, and realized that the sounds were voices coming from within the shed at his back. As he reached over to shake Sandy he looked down at his wrist watch. It was after five.

"I don't think you should have done it, Ted." The unintelligible mumbling suddenly resolved into understandable speech. The owner of the voice must have drawn near the wall against which the boys leaned. "Not with the trouble we've been having lately," the same voice added.

"But, Dad," another voice replied protestingly, "when I wrote to Ken the last time everything seemed all right. We hadn't had any of our pots robbed for weeks. How was I to know that Jackson would start acting up again just now?"

"I know." The older man's voice was worried but insistent. "It wasn't your fault. But I wish . . ."

"Ken and his friend can take care of themselves, Dad."

"Maybe so. But I don't like to put guests in a position where they have to 'take care of themselves.'" A car door slammed. "Well, it's too late now. We'll just have to be especially careful while they're here—careful not to get into any sort of a row with Jackson. So long as we keep our mouths shut, I suppose he will too— and there needn't be any reason for your friends to be involved at all."

A car engine started up and gears clashed. The small truck backed out of the shed, its hind end barely in the boys' view. Then it reversed its direction and disappeared again, heading toward the pier some yards beyond.

Ken couldn't make himself meet Sandy's eyes, but he finally raised his head. "I wonder . . ." he began in his most innocent voice.

"Peace and quiet!" Sandy said explosively under his breath. "Yes, sir! There's nothing like a little seaside village for peace and quiet!"

CHAPTER II

MR. JACKSON GETS WET

"WE'RE IN A BAD SPOT," Ken said thoughtfully, after a moment of silence.

"We usually are." Sandy half got to his feet and then, seeing that Ken hadn't moved, dropped down on the grass again.

"If we're a nuisance to the Batesons," Ken went on, "—and judging from what we heard we seem to be— we ought to leave."

"But we can't very well turn right around and go home without giving some excuse," Sandy pointed out, his mood now as serious as Ken's. "Unless, of course," he added, "you want to admit we overheard that conversation."

Ken shook his head. "That would embarrass them." He hauled himself to his feet. "Let's go and say hello."

"We can always phone Pop and tell him to wire us to come home," Sandy suggested. He, too, was erect now, but he was taking the time to brush off the seat of his trousers. "What do you suppose it's all about, anyway?" he muttered. "He talked about having 'pots robbed.' Aren't lobster traps called 'pots'?"

Ken nodded, grinning faintly. "Look who's curious now!" Then he motioned his redheaded friend forward toward the corner of the shed. "We'd better not start nosing around," he added quietly as they stepped out on the driveway. "It's probably nothing serious, but if they don't want us in on it, that's their business."

"Oh, sure." There was a defensive note in Sandy's voice. "They're your friends, of course, anyway. Whatever you say—"

"Oh, cut it out!" Ken told him. But he knew that Sandy would follow his lead now. Maybe, he thought, as they headed down toward the pier, Ted would tell him frankly what the trouble was, and then they would know what was best to do.

The two fishing boats that had just been tied up, one behind the other, were identical so far as the boys could tell. Each was about thirty-five feet long, and had a cabin occupying its forward half, rimmed by a narrow catwalk on either side. Where the cabin ended amidships a short, stubby mast reared some fifteen feet into the air, fitted with a boom complete with pulleys and assorted tackle. A wheel and motor controls were attached to the cabin wall, under a small protecting roof, and the aft part of each boat was bare except for a winch on the starboard side directly behind the cabin door.

Even before they had noted these details, they saw the four men—all dressed alike in overalls and high hip boots. Two were loading tubs onto the truck that had just been driven out of the shed. The other two —one on each boat—were hosing down the aft decks.

"Hi!" One of the boat-washers had looked up. His

heavy boots thumped on the pier as he ran to meet them. "Hi, Ken! Glad you got here." His tanned face was split wide in a welcoming grin.

"Hi yourself, Ted!"

They pumped each other's hands enthusiastically.

"When'd you get in?" Ted Bateson demanded.

"Just long enough ago to eat some of your mother's sandwiches." Ken, too, was grinning. "Ted, this is Sandy Allen. Sandy—Ted."

"Hi," Sandy said. "It was swell of you to let me come along."

Ted, ignoring this, had taken a step backward and was looking Sandy up and down. "Glad to meet you," he said finally, and two huge hands met in a firm grip. "You weren't kidding about him, were you, Ken?" Ted went on. "He wrote," he explained to Sandy, "that you were built just like me—but twice as tall."

"Not quite." Sandy laughed. "You're not exactly what I'd call a pygmy."

"Alongside of you I am." Ted narrowed his dark eyes thoughtfully. "Two hundred?"

"Just about," Sandy admitted.

"Then between us we ought to be able to keep him in line." Ted pounded Ken's shoulder.

"You can try," Ken said calmly. But a moment later he was smiling again. He had been pretty sure his two friends would like each other, but witnessing the proof was pleasant.

"Here they are, Dad!" Ted called out then, and one of the men who had been loading the truck put down his burden to join them. "Ken Holt and Sandy Allen," Ted explained. "My father."

"How do you do, sir."

"Glad to meet you, Mr. Bateson."

"And I'm mighty glad to meet both of you." Bateson was an older replica of his son, with a skin weathered by salt spray and hair as silvered as the shingles on the shed. And—whatever concern their arrival had caused him—his voice was as warmly welcoming as Ted's. "We've all been looking forward to having you out here. Ted's been talking of nothing else."

He turned toward his son. "I'll take the lobsters over to the fish company tonight. Maybe Ken and Sandy will like to look over the boats while you finish up."

"O.K. Thanks, Dad." He raised his voice. "Hank! Come here and meet some friends of mine."

The man who had been helping with the loading turned his head slowly and walked as slowly toward them, pausing on the way to send a stream of tobacco juice over the side of the dock. He was older than Mr. Bateson, and taller and leaner. He looked as if he had been soaking in salt water for a good many years.

When Ted had made the introductions, Hank Bower shifted his cud before he drawled a slow, "Hello, boys."

Mr. Bateson smiled. "Hank's forgotten more about sailing and fishing than most people ever knew," he confided. "I think he was born in a fish net."

"Ain't so much to know *or* forget," Hank said laconically. "Fish—and water—you can mostly figure out far enough ahead of time what they're fixin' to do to head off any real trouble. They're not like—"

"We'd better get those lobsters moving, Hank," Mr. Bateson broke in. He started toward the truck, and

Hank, with a nod, followed after him. "See you at the house, boys," Mr. Bateson called back.

"There's just one more of us to meet," Ted said, leading the way down the dock. "And the boats, of course. That's the *Mary Bateson* down there," he pointed. "And this is the one I run." He stopped alongside the first sturdy craft. "The *Traveler*, we call her. And this is my crew, Tim Bower—Hank's son."

Thin and bright-eyed, Tim wiped his wet hands on his overalls before he greeted them. "I'm sure glad to see you," he said with a grin that flashed sidewise at Ted.

"He isn't just being polite," Ted said. "He's been wanting to take a week off to get his sailboat in shape before winter—and I've been telling him that if you two would take his place, it would be O.K."

Ken flashed a quick look at Sandy, but Sandy was studying the top of the *Traveler's* blunt mast.

"Well," Ken said slowly, "I—" Tim's grin was fading. "I don't know how useful we'd be," Ken hurried on. "We don't know much about boats, and we know less about the lobster business."

"Oh, it's a cinch," Tim assured him. "Ted will tell you just what to do. He's a very bossy guy." He evaded Ted's lunging fist and added, "Seriously, he's the brains of this outfit. All he needs are a couple of extra muscles to help haul the pots aboard and drop them over again."

"With that flattering recommendation, how can you refuse?" Ted grinned at Ken and Sandy. "We'll call you tonight, Tim," he added, "when we've had a chance to talk it over. Maybe they'd rather just loaf around."

"Sure." Tim was suddenly embarrassed, as if he felt he had sounded too urgent. "Everything's clean. You want me to check those plugs?"

"I'll do it," Ted answered.

A few minutes later, when Tim had gone, Ted was proudly showing Ken and Sandy over the *Traveler*.

"And this is the cabin," he said, after they had looked at the deck equipment. "Come on in and look around while I check that number six plug. I think she's fouled up."

They followed him into the tiny room. The next moment Ted was almost out of sight in the engine compartment. The boys bent down to see what he was doing to the heavy piece of machinery that extended under the aft deck. It was a big eight-cylinder engine and the plug that Ted was removing was located almost six feet behind the cabin. When he backed out of the cramped space he brought it with him.

"Points too close," he muttered, squinting at it. He took a feeler gauge from a box of tools and adjusted the spark gap. "That's better. I'll be through in a jiffy now."

When he disappeared for the second time the boys glanced around the small compact cabin. There were four bunks, two on each side. And up forward, where the bow narrowed down almost to a point, there was a small galley complete with a gasoline stove and a sink. A small ice chest stood under the sink, and Sandy, who could never resist an icebox, opened its door.

"We'll do fine," he said, turning to smile at Ken. "Ham, cheese, milk . . ." His face sobered. "I forgot. We probably won't—"

He didn't finish the sentence. Ted was already crawling out of the engine compartment.

"How do you like her?" Ted asked. He bent down to shut off the main valve on the gasoline line and then wiped his hands on a piece of waste.

"Pretty neat," Sandy said admiringly. "Especially the kitchen."

"Galley, you mean," Ted corrected. He smiled. "We keep it pretty well stocked. Lobstering is hard work and you need plenty of food to—or am I scaring you off?" He spoke earnestly. "It isn't really a matter of life and death with Tim, you know. If you don't feel like coming out with me . . ."

"We don't scare very easily." Ken's voice too was earnest, and he was looking directly at Ted.

There was a moment's silence in the little cabin, and then Ted said, "That's what I thought—from what I've been reading about you two lately. In fact, that's why I thought—I mean, I was wondering—" He broke off abruptly, and threw the handful of waste he was still holding into the engine compartment. "We'd better get up to the house and get cleaned up for supper."

Ken, conscious of Sandy's watchful eye, asked quietly, "That's why you thought what? What were you wondering?"

Ted shook his head. "I guess I meant wandering," he said with an attempt at a laugh. Then he moved to one of the bunks, leaned over, and straightened again with a rifle in his hand—a .22 caliber pump gun. He emptied its magazine into his hand and dropped the cartridges into a box on a shelf over the bunk. "Let's go."

With Ted briskly leading the way they climbed out on the aft deck and Ted closed the cabin door.

"What's the rifle for?" Ken asked.

Ted evaded his questioning look. "Oh—just to play around with. We throw cans overboard and shoot at them for target practice."

"With extra long bullets?"

"Just happened to have them around."

Ted leaped up on the dock—and stopped there abruptly. Behind him the boys waited, Ken with one foot on the low rail that ran around the aft deck, his hand grasping the dock piling.

After a long pause Ted took one step forward.

"What are you doing on this dock?" he demanded, his voice low in his throat.

The voice that answered him was harsh.

"Just came around to tell your old man to keep his opinions to himself. If he knows what's good for him, he'll stop calling people lobster pirates unless he can make the charge stick."

Ken moved far enough along the rail to be able to step up beside Ted, and an instant later Sandy joined them.

Ted didn't even glance at them. He was standing rigidly, staring straight at the man facing him some fifteen feet away.

"Get off this dock, Jackson," Ted said slowly.

"When I'm ready." The man's face was rough with stubble, his head was thrust a little forward, and his arms hung slightly away from his sides. They seemed too long for the square, heavy body.

"Get off now," Ted said. "And stay off."

"You going to make me?" The harsh voice broke on a laugh, and he gestured toward the rifle in the crook of Ted's arm. "With that thing to help, maybe."

Ted dropped the rifle and took a step forward.

Jackson rushed him immediately, flailing out with both arms. Ted stopped a slow haymaker with his left forearm and drove a short chop to Jackson's jaw. Again Jackson's arms flailed, and again Ted landed a swift right, to the nose this time. Immediately afterward he ducked beneath that long left arm and then spun around, to avoid backing up against the piled lobster traps.

Before he had completed the turn Jackson delivered a blow to Ted's chest. The brute power behind it almost lifted the boy off his feet, and he staggered as he tried to side-step the follow-up.

But just as Ted regained his balance, his rubber boot slid on a patch of water and he went down. Immediately Jackson launched a vicious kick at the prone figure. And, as Ted twisted away from him, the man raised his foot again.

Sandy broke swiftly from Ken's firm grasp on his arm. Before the man's foot could complete its second arc Sandy had leaped forward and pinned those long arms to Jackson's side, Then, using his knee as a fulcrum, Sandy half-lifted, half-dragged the burly figure away from Ted and threw it across the dock. Jackson skidded several feet and landed hard against the piled lobster pots.

"Dirty fighting!" Sandy said.

Jackson hauled himself immediately to a sitting position, all his rage now transferred to the redheaded giant standing over him. As he groped for support to pull himself erect, his hands came in contact with a boat hook. Suddenly he was up and charging toward Sandy, the huge hook thrust forward like a spear.

"Look out!" Ted shouted.

Ken did the only thing there was time to do. He stuck his foot out into Jackson's path.

The lunging figure stumbled and fell. The boat hook flew out of his hand. In a kind of slow motion the heavy body slid forward over the dock to come to rest at Sandy's feet.

Sandy didn't hesitate. He grasped the slack of the tough overalls Jackson was wearing, and his back muscles heaved. For an instant Sandy held the man in the air, those long arms dangling, before he swung in a half circle and let go. Jackson seemed to float briefly in space—and then he hit the water with a splash that sent spray flying.

He came up quickly, in the center of a patch of foam. But he didn't attempt to climb back on the dock. Snarling words of unintelligible rage over his shoulder, he struck out for the near-by shore.

"That's too bad," Ted said slowly as they watched the thrashing arms carrying Jackson away. "He's a nasty character." He was absent-mindedly rubbing the arm where Jackson's first blow had landed, and he seemed to be speaking almost to himself.

"It's especially too bad that it happened right now. Dad didn't want—" He stopped abruptly, as if suddenly aware of the fact that he was talking aloud.

"Isn't it about time you finished one of those sentences?" Ken asked, taking Ted's unbruised arm and turning him toward the house. "Let's go call Tim and tell him he can have the week off. What do you say?"

He was speaking to Ted, but he looked at Sandy as he voiced the question.

Sandy gave him a nod and a wink. "*I* say yes," he said firmly.

CHAPTER III

KEN AND SANDY SIGN ON

OUT IN THE KITCHEN Mrs. Bateson was clearing up the supper dishes. In the dining room Mr. Bateson filled the air with blue smoke from his pipe and looked soberly at Ken and Sandy across the big, round, old-fashioned table. Ted sat beside his father, silently thoughtful.

The boys had just admitted overhearing the conversation in the shed.

"Our first reaction was that we ought to clear out," Ken explained. "And of course we'll still go—tonight, if you say so—if it's really awkward for you to have us here now. But—"

"It's certainly not awkward for us," Mr. Bateson cut in, echoing Ken's word with a wry smile. "In fact, I'd say it might have been pretty awkward for Ted if you *hadn't* been around this afternoon. But I don't trust Jackson, and I wouldn't like to be responsible for anything happening to either of you boys—"

It was Sandy's turn to cut in. "We can take care of ourselves, Mr. Bateson, if that's all that's worrying you.

But it certainly burns me up to see a man getting away with the kind of stuff you've been telling us about. If you and all the other lobstermen are sure that Jackson is robbing your traps—well, can't something be done about him? Can't we help you do something?"

"Being sure and being able to prove it are two different things," Ted said quietly.

"You mean you've never been able to catch him with the lobsters in his possession?" Sandy asked.

"Unfortunately lobsters don't have serial numbers—or any other means of identification," Mr. Bateson explained with a smile. "If Jackson comes in with a couple of hundred pounds in his hold, nobody can prove that they didn't all come from his own pots."

"But can't you guard the traps?" Sandy queried.

Ted and his father exchanged a glance.

"You know," Ken said to Sandy, "I have the feeling that every time we open our mouths around here we expose our ignorance." And when the Batesons allowed their carefully restrained smiles to break through, he hurried on.

"It's true," Ken said, "that we don't know a thing about lobstering—though Sandy, of course, has known a good many lobsters personally, once they've been broiled and put in front of him on a platter."

"Why should you know the techniques of our business?" Mr. Bateson pointed out, sober again. "Very few people know anything about it, except working lobstermen like ourselves. Ted and I were just smiling because—well, because we haven't had much to smile over lately."

"That's the point," Ken said earnestly. "We can see

that you've got trouble enough on your hands right now. And we don't want to add to it by hanging around if we're in the way. But if there's any chance that we could be useful—if there's anything at all we could do—"

"That's for me too," Sandy cut in.

"If it's O.K. with Dad," Ted said suddenly, leaning forward, "I vote we take you up on that."

He waited a moment, looking at his father, and Mr. Bateson finally nodded.

"If you'll make sure, Ted," he told his son, "that they don't tangle with Jackson again. He's tricky and mean."

"As I see it," Ken said briskly, in a tone suggesting that everything was settled and they could now get down to facts, "the point is not to tangle with him but to put a stop to these thefts."

"Right," Ted agreed. "But you'll see why it's not easy. The reason we grinned at Sandy's suggestion of guarding the traps, for example, is that they're scattered over some ten miles of ocean."

"Wow!" Sandy murmured. "And I suppose he goes out at night."

"And it's impossible to try to follow him," Ted went on, anticipating their next suggestion. "He'd hear the sound of our motor and just stay away from our traps that night. And in the meantime we'd be using up a lot of gas we can't afford. So he pretty much takes what he wants—and we have to let him."

"It's not quite that hopeless," Mr. Bateson put in. "You see, we—all the lobstermen around here—sell most of our catch to wholesale fishhouses. The wholesalers are our friends, and they know Jackson as well as we do. So they refuse to buy from him. Consequently, Jackson has to get rid of his lobsters in any way he can—usually at about half the standard price."

Sandy shook his head. "I don't get this. He has to go out after them, the same way you would yourself. Why is it worth his while if he only gets half price in the end?"

"I've often asked myself that same question," Bateson agreed. "Of course he doesn't bait the traps, which is a certain amount of work and expense. And he doesn't own the traps—and they represent a considerable investment. He does have a few of his own," he added.

"Just enough to give him an excuse to go out," Ted said disgustedly.

"Can't the government do anything about him?" Ken wanted to know. "You have to have some sort of license to trap lobsters, don't you?"

Mr. Bateson nodded over the match he was applying to his pipe. "We're all licensed. And we're each assigned a buoy color to mark our own traps. But for the Coast Guard to catch Jackson in the act—" He shrugged. "They'd need a special patrol to watch him. And Jackson would just behave himself until the patrol was withdrawn."

"They've already tried it," Ted pointed out. "They've had night patrols out, but so far Jackson's been too smart for them. Maybe they'll get him eventually, of course—"

"But in the meantime you take a licking," Sandy finished.

"That's about it, son," Mr. Bateson said.

"Here's Paul Anthony, Dan."

They all looked up at the sound of Mrs. Bateson's voice from the kitchen, and an instant later a tall, thin man walked through the low doorway. His bald head gleamed in the lamplight.

"Oh! Sorry," he said abruptly, as he appeared. "I didn't know you had company."

"Come on in, Paul." Mr. Bateson gestured with his pipe. He introduced the boys and added, quietly, that they had just been discussing Jackson.

Anthony sat down heavily. "Well, that's what I'm here about—as usual," he grunted. "Got hit again last night. Hauled a hundred and thirty pots today—for a total of eighty pounds. More than half the pots had been emptied before I got there."

"Our story's about the same," Bateson told him. I didn't do so badly, but Ted's line wasn't worth a plugged nickel."

"Look, Bateson," Anthony said, putting his hands on his knees and leaning forward, "I know I'm a newcomer in this business, and probably don't have the patience of you old-timers. But I'm getting sick and tired of this."

Bateson smiled faintly. "And what do you suggest we do?"

"I don't know exactly," Anthony admitted. "I know you say setting a guard—or following him—won't get us anywhere. But"—he brought his hand down on the table so hard it quivered—"I'm willing to spend a good deal to get rid of Jackson. One way or the other," he added grimly.

"Take it easy, Paul," Bateson advised. "He'll be tripped up sooner or later."

"But probably not before I go broke," Anthony said explosively. "How long can *you* keep this up?"

"I don't know." Bateson shrugged. "But I can't afford nightly patrols, either. Look, Paul: we've had lobster pirates occasionally in the past, and managed to survive. The man's already pretty well ostracized by everybody in Eastend—maybe he'll get tired of that and leave of his own accord. Or one of these fine nights the Coast Guard will catch him. You'll see."

Anthony got to his feet. "I can't figure you out, Dan. You've got more at stake than I have—you and the other old-timers around here. I'm just an ex-restaurant owner who got into the business more or less for my health. And yet I'm the only one who seems to want action."

"Maybe we've had more time to learn there isn't much we can do, Paul."

Anthony turned back from the kitchen door. "Isn't much you will do, you mean. Sure, I know you carry a rifle on your boats, like I do. But maybe I'm not going to be quite so particular as the rest of you about waiting for absolute proof before I use it. Good night," he added abruptly. "Glad to have met you boys." And then he was gone.

"Poor Paul," Bateson said soberly. "I'm afraid he did sink all his money into lobstering after all—and without knowing much about it."

"Was he really a restaurant man?" Sandy asked. "Seems a strange background for lobstering."

"Not so very," Ted said. "He used to own the Live Lobster, a famous sea food place. So maybe it seemed a natural switch, when his health went bad. Anyway," he added to his father, "I don't feel so sorry for him. He usually gets enough of a catch to fill his restaurant order." He turned to the boys. "He sells to the new owners of his old place and gets a mighty fancy price too."

"And you boys will get mighty little sleep if you expect to be up at five in the morning," Mrs. Bateson said suddenly from the kitchen door. "Look at the time."

Her husband glanced at Sandy and Ken. "You're sure—?" He stopped. They hadn't told Mrs. Bateson of the fight on the dock, and he apparently didn't want to refer to Jackson's new aggressive tactics in front of her.

"We're sure we want to go along," Ken said quickly. "If you can trust Sandy not to eat the catch as soon as it's hauled in."

"Don't worry." Ted grinned. "He'll be too busy—" He stopped. "Gosh! I forgot to call Tim and tell him he can get to work on that sailboat." He dashed for the telephone.

Half an hour later Ken and Sandy stood looking through their bedroom window out over the harbor. A few lights twinkled in the distance, their reflections shimmering on the still water, and from the inlet the harbor light blinked solemnly on and off.

"Ted said that Jackson's dock is the fourth one down from here," Sandy said thoughtfully. "It's probably visible from some window in this house. So why can't somebody just keep an eye on it and see if he sneaks off in the night? What would be so hard about that?"

"If he were followed he wouldn't take anything— and they'd have wasted the gas," Ken reminded him. "It's a matter of practical economics, I guess."

"Sure. But—" Outraged justice raised Sandy's voice.

"Keep it quiet," Ken cautioned him. "You'll wake everybody up."

"Oh—" Sandy gestured disgustedly and turned to throw himself on the bed. "When I think of that—"

"Turn out the light," Ken said suddenly from the window, his voice taut.

Sandy flipped the switch of the bed lamp and sprang instantly to his feet. "What's up?" he asked, rejoining Ken at the window.

"Thought I saw someone. Listen."

From across the harbor came the muted noise of a car. But in the near neighborhood of the Bateson house no other sound seemed to be audible except the chirp of crickets.

Sandy had already begun to turn back toward the bed when Ken grabbed his arm. "Look!"

A shadowy figure was moving silently down the Bateson drive toward the dock. Just beyond the shed it melted into the darkness. One hollow footstep betrayed a heel let down on the wooden planking, and then again all was still.

"Come on," Ken said. "Let's take a look."

Hastily they pulled trousers on over their pajamas and thrust their feet into sneakers.

"Shall we call Ted?" Sandy whispered.

"Let's see what it is first. Don't want them to think we're crazy—and maybe we are."

"Would Jackson try to damage their boats?" Sandy asked, pausing at the door.

"I shouldn't think so. He'd want them in good shape

to set the traps every day. Unless," he added, "this afternoon made him so mad he forgets what side his bread is buttered on."

They opened their door quietly and Ken led the way down the carpeted stairs and through the darkened house. They moved swiftly along in the grass and paused, finally, in the shadow of the shed to listen. Once again only the crickets broke the silence.

Then, even more cautiously, they walked down the dock itself to stand in the protection of the piled lobster pots.

The water lapped softly at the pilings, and the boats were rocking in the swell of the gentle tide. Several yards out a fish leaped suddenly above the surface— and the boys started.

"Exhaust fumes," Sandy whispered, after a long moment had gone by unbroken by any sound or sudden movement.

Ken nodded. "Could a boat have just left here?" he breathed. "Without our hearing?"

Sandy tensed. "Watch that light," he murmured, gesturing toward the inlet blinker.

Ken turned toward it. An instant later the light flashed again, and in the momentary gleam they could see the silhouette of a boat heading through the inlet. It was a long boat—that much they could see—and it seemed to have no mast. Its engine must have been entirely silent, because they could not hear even the faintest sound.

"Jackson?" Sandy suggested.

"Didn't look like a lobster boat."

They waited, but in the next flash the boat was already only a half-seen shadow, and it did not appear again. After several long minutes of vigil they gave up and went back to their room.

"We shouldn't try to invent trouble out of nothing," Ken said quietly as they settled down on the beds. "It may have been some friend of the Batesons' just borrowing their dock long enough to take on water or something—and not wanting to disturb them when he knew they'd be asleep."

Sandy raised himself on one elbow and looked across the dimness toward Ken. "You feel all right?"

"Sure. Why?"

"Because there's something wrong with your head. Why should anybody borrow this dock when there's a town dock, with lights and everything, a quarter of a mile away?"

"I don't know why he should," Ken admitted.

"There's something fishy going on around here—and I'm not trying to make jokes."

"You're sure of that, huh?" Ken's voice was muffled.

"Sure I'm sure of it."

"You don't think we should forget the whole business?"

"Are you crazy?" Sandy sat up straight.

"No. Just cautious. Be sure you remember this conversation the next time you tell me *I* always get us into messes. This one—"

Sandy's pillow, accurately thrown, drowned out the rest of the sentence.

CHAPTER IV

MEETING IN THE FOG

THE FOG was so heavy at five thirty the next morning
that Ken and Sandy had to go halfway down the dock
before they could recognize the three dim figures moving about at its tip as Ted, his father, and Hank Bower.

"Thought maybe you'd changed your minds," Ted
said with a grin as they approached.

"We got up when you called us," Ken told him. "But
we seem to have more thumbs than usual at this hour
in the morning—especially in the kitchen."

Mr. Bateson bent down to loosen the *Mary Bateson's*
bow line. "You're in good time," he assured the boys.
"Hank and I have to get out before the *Traveler* can
leave, anyway."

"Could you wait just a minute, sir?" Ken asked.

When Mr. Bateson nodded, Ken launched quickly
into the story of the shadowy figure they had seen the
night before, and the boat that slipped so silently past
the inlet light.

Both the Batesons and Hank listened without comment.

When Ken had finished, Mr. Bateson said thoughtfully, "Strange. Didn't notice any signs of a prowler when we came out this morning. Might have been the Coast Guard cutter, I suppose."

"Nope." Hank's single syllable was definite. "They'd have heard that."

"Anyway," Ted put in, "why would the Coast Guard cutter have put in here at that hour?"

His father shrugged. "You're sure you did see all this?" he asked the boys. "The light out here is likely to be deceptive, you know, and—"

"We both saw the boat," Ken answered. "*And* the man."

"And smelled the exhaust fumes," Sandy added.

Mr. Bateson gestured to Hank, who jumped aboard the *Mary Bateson* and caught the rope Mr. Bateson threw him.

While he was coiling it neatly on deck Mr. Bateson said, "Well, it might have been anybody—just putting in for a minute, for some reason. But since they don't seem to have done any harm, there's no reason why we should worry about it," he added. Then he started the engine and in a moment smoke belched from the muffler that reached into the air alongside the mast.

Hank lifted a boat hook from the deck and dug its point into the piling of the dock, and as the *Mary Bateson's* stern swung away he jerked the hook free and dropped it again. When the boat's stern was pointed into the harbor, Mr. Bateson opened the throttle a little. The throbbing exhaust increased its pitch, and white foam broke under the stern as the screw caught hold. The *Mary Bateson* began to back away. A moment later Mr.

Bateson swung the wheel hard over, the propeller reversed, and she swung around.

As she began to melt into the mist Mr. Bateson's voice floated back to them. "You're taking the number five line today, Ted. Be careful out there."

"I guess he does think we're crazy," Ken said.

"No, he doesn't," Ted assured him. "But this is kind of an informal place—people borrow each other's docks and stuff. I guess it really might have been almost anybody."

"I suppose you're right." Ken thrust the whole thing out of his mind. "What do we do first?"

"Get aboard and get into hip boots." Ted tossed the stern and bow lines onto the *Traveler's* deck and jumped lightly after them.

When the boys had joined him he pressed the starter button and listened to the engine's answering rumble. "Good," he muttered. "Hitting on all eight."

He glanced over the side to make sure the *Traveler* was clear, then put the wheel over to starboard and kicked the lever into reverse. The sturdy boat came alive with vibration as the engine took up the load. Ted kept the wheel over until her bow pointed out into the harbor, then put it into forward speed and opened the throttle. The *Traveler* shuddered and began to move ahead.

In a moment the dock had disappeared from view and she was moving in a world of impenetrable mist.

"How do you know where you're going?" Sandy asked, when he and Ken had come on deck again in the heavy boots Ted had told them to put on.

"Quiet," Ted commanded. He was a suddenly authoritative figure, standing quietly at the wheel. "We steer by ear in this pea soup."

He threw the clutch out and let the engine idle as the boat glided smoothly ahead. From the left somewhere came the faint sound of voices. Ted swung the wheel until the bow pointed in that direction, and then engaged the clutch again. After another hundred feet he threw it into neutral once more.

The voices were closer now, and more distinct, and there was an occasional clang of metal.

"Climb up forward, Sandy," Ted ordered, "and keep an eye out for a dock. It should be dead ahead." His own eyes were peering intently over the cabin roof.

"Straight ahead!" Sandy called out almost immediately, as the heavy end pilings of a large pier suddenly materialized out of the fog. "Only about fifty feet!"

Ted slammed the gears into reverse and the *Traveler* lost its forward motion with a convulsive shudder. Then he swung the bow to starboard and edged the craft slowly ahead again. The bulkhead slid past. When the *Traveler* was motionless alongside the dock he disengaged the gears.

There was another boat directly in front of them. The letters on her squat stern spelled out *Stingray*.

"Ahoy *Stingray!*" Ted called out.

"Be out of here in a minute," the answer came back, from a misty figure on her deck.

"Right. That's Anthony's boat," Ted told the boys.

A moment later Anthony himself appeared on his aft deck, almost close enough to reach over and shake hands. "I'm ready, Ted. Will you give me a little room?"

The *Traveler* backed off to allow the *Stingray's* stern

to swing away from the pier, and as Anthony moved off into the fog Ted urged his boat forward into the vacated place.

"Sixty gallons ought to do it," he said to a figure on the dock as the hose from a gasoline pump was handed over to him.

"Sixty it is," the man answered. "You're a little late," he added conversationally as the fuel flowed through the distended hose. "Your dad's come and gone."

"I know." Ted looked up at him. "And our friend?"

"Oh, him!" The pump attendant's voice was suddenly scornful. "He filled up last night when he came in." He looked at the meter and shut off the pump. "Too bad I can't refuse to sell him gas." He accepted the hose Ted handed up, scribbled something in a little book, and gave it to Ted for his signature. "What about oil?"

"I've got a couple gallons aboard." Ted snapped the engine into life. "Well—I'll be seeing you."

"Look out!" Ken shouted an instant later, from the stern, as the bow of an incoming boat suddenly sprang into view.

Ted shot the *Traveler* forward, and the newcomer as quickly reversed, but even so the two craft came within inches of collision.

"Darn fool!" Ted swung the *Traveler* in a tight circle. "Coming in that fast in a fog!"

Ken swallowed hard and waited a moment for the image of the onrushing boat to fade from his mind. "Who was it?"

Ted's face was still set, and his eyes angry, as he moved into the clear water beyond the dock. "Jackson."

The heavy bong of a bell buoy almost directly ahead seemed to echo the single sharp word.

"I thought Jackson fueled up last night," Sandy said.

"That's right." Ted steered around the heaving buoy. "Which means he was probably at our pots again, or he wouldn't need more fuel this morning." He studied the compass momentarily and twisted the wheel to head due north. "You're sure it wasn't his boat you saw last night?"

Ken nodded. "His boat's pretty much like this one. The one we saw was a long, low baby—with no mast and no noise."

"Oh, well . . ." Ted seemed to give himself a shake. "How about some coffee to warm us up?" It was clear he wanted to forget about Jackson for a while.

"Swell," Sandy said. "I'll make it."

"Know how to get a gasoline stove going?" Ted asked.

"Sure." Sandy was already at the cabin door.

"There's coffee in a can over the stove."

When Sandy had disappeared Ken moved to stand alongside Ted, who was peering forward into the fog as if by sheer will power he could penetrate that gray curtain.

"Where're we going now?" Ken asked.

"To get bait." Ted took one hand off the wheel and opened a chart. "See," he said, pointing to the narrow harbor inlet. "We'll be going through in a minute. You'll feel it."

A moment later the *Traveler's* bow lifted and dipped. Ted opened the throttle wide and she surged ahead through the swells that had begun to strike them regularly.

"Hey!" Sandy called from below. "How am I supposed to hold the pot on the stove with you rocking the boat?"

"It'll stay there," Ted called back. "Don't worry about it." He pointed to the chart again. "We're in the bay now—cutting right across to here." His finger indicated a small harbor opposite Eastend. "We get our bunkers there."

"Bunkers?" Ken repeated questioningly. "What are they?"

Ted grinned. "You'll know when you get near enough. They're a small fish—very fat and very smelly. Soap factories buy 'em for grease, but they're good bait too."

"There's some very nice ham in the icebox," Sandy said suddenly from the door. "How about a sandwich?"

"That's an idea," Ted agreed.

"But we just had breakfast before—" Ken began. But Sandy had already disappeared. "If he gets seasick and can't eat," he added to Ted, "it'll be the greatest tragedy that could happen to him."

"You'll be hungry pretty soon yourself out here."

"I am already. But don't tell him."

Ted checked the compass again. "Take the wheel, will you, Ken? I want to get the baskets ready."

"Sure. But what do I do with it?"

"Keep her heading the way she's going—north by the compass. And don't worry." Ted grinned. "There's nothing in front of you except five miles of water."

Ken touched the spokes gingerly but discovered after

a few moments that it wasn't difficult to keep the *Traveler* on her course. There was no wind to pull her to port or starboard.

Behind him, Ted had opened a hatchway in the deck and dropped down into the shallow hold to grope for the steel mesh bait baskets. When he had lifted out four of them he climbed back on deck and closed the hatch.

"O.K. I'll take her now."

Ken yielded his place at the wheel.

Ted listened intently a moment and then throttled the motor down. From somewhere ahead came the sound of a whistling buoy, its eerie note rising and falling as the water lifted and fell in its steel tube.

"Right on the nose." Ted pointed to the buoy's position on the chart. "Halfway there now."

"Chow," Sandy announced triumphantly, thrusting a plate of thick sandwiches through the cabin doorway into Ken's hands. When he reappeared the next time he had three steaming mugs of coffee. "Do we have to feed you, Ted?"

"I wouldn't trust you." Ted slipped a loop of rope over the spokes of the wheel and cut to half speed. "There. She'll hold her course while we eat."

It was half past six when they pulled up to a dock where several bunker boats were busy unloading. Ted handed up his baskets and received them back full of the bunkers caught fresh a few hours earlier, but already filling the air with a strong odor.

By the time Sandy had finished cleaning up the galley Ted had backed off and was heading southeast toward the end of the bay and the open sea beyond. The swell was striking them from the side now, and the

Traveler rolled enough to set the baskets of fish sliding on the deck.

Ted handed the wheel to Ken again. "Keep her as she is until we pick up the bell buoy."

"Aye, aye, sir."

Then Ted went briefly into the cabin and reappeared with a hank of twine and what looked like an oversize needle.

He perched himself on a narrow rail, oblivious to the boat's rolling motion, and threaded the end of the twine through the needle.

"Here's a job for you, Sandy—if you don't mind the smell."

"I can stand anything you can. What do I do?"

"This." Ted began to string the small fish on the line. When some twenty of them were dangling there, he grouped them in bunches of four or five and cut the twine between each cluster. Then he tied each short line, so that the fish were slung in a loop. "We hook one bunch in each trap," he explained, threading the needle again. "I'll string 'em. You tie the bunches."

"O.K." Sandy studied Ted's casual position on the rail a moment, and then moved forward to climb up beside him.

At that instant the *Traveler* dipped heavily, and Sandy clutched at air.

Ted grabbed him and thrust him back.

"Maybe you better sit on the deck," he suggested with a grin, "until you get your sea legs."

Sandy gulped and looked at the heaving water. "I think maybe you're right."

When the first harsh sounds of a bell reached them,

some twenty minutes later, Ted left his perch and took over the wheel. He shut down the throttle and eased carefully past the buoy, then shoved the throttle forward again and returned the wheel to Ken.

"Hold her steady," he said. "We have another half-hour's run at least."

The motion of the boat changed once more as they began to take the swells head on. Sandy, more confident, was soon sitting easily on the rail. And as his fingers became adept at handling the slippery twine he began to tie the bunches as swiftly as Ted could thread the line. Ken, too, had relaxed at the wheel.

But Ted seemed to grow uneasy as the time slipped smoothly by. He lifted his head more and more often, to peer intently into the still-heavy mist.

"She should be lifting by now," he muttered as they finished stringing the bait. Crossing over to the wheel he pressed a button near it, and the *Traveler's* horn suddenly shattered the quiet. "Give her a blast about every thirty seconds," he told Ken. "You never can tell what other boats might be near us. These are busy waters."

He opened the deck hatch again and lifted up four round tubs which he began to fill with sea water from a hose.

"What do you do if the fog doesn't lift?" Sandy asked.

"Go back home. It'd take too long to find the pots in a mess like this."

"Does it happen often," Ken asked, "that you have to waste gas on a trip that—" He broke off to sound the *Traveler's* signal once again.

Immediately, and almost dead ahead of them, another horn sounded in answer.

Ted dropped his hose and leaped for the wheel, one finger jabbing at the horn button. As he threw the clutch out and cut the engine the answer came again, as if rising from the water almost beneath their bow.

They could hear the quiet purr of the other boat's engine now, when the horn's blast died.

"Not a lobster boat. Twin-engine job—underwater exhaust," Ted muttered, cocking his head to concentrate on the soft gurgling sound.

"There it is!" Sandy said.

The dark bulk emerging from the soupy atmosphere was coming forward very slowly. Her knife-edged bow split the water cleanly.

A head in a gleaming yellow sou'wester materialized on the enclosed bridge, and a hand waved to signify that the *Traveler* had been sighted. Then the soft purr of the twin engines died completely away, and the two boats drifted toward each other in silence.

"What a boat!" Sandy murmured.

She was about forty feet long and all black. There was a small open cockpit up forward and a larger one aft, but the rest of her lean length was cabin—long, low, and streamlined. The windshield of the bridge was sloped like that on a racing car. As she drew abreast of the *Traveler* her skipper left the wheel to appear in the rear cockpit, where he was joined by a man in white ducks.

Across the twenty feet that separated the two craft the men were clearly visible. The skipper was tall and thin, the other man short and plump with sandy hair.

"Little thick out here today," the skipper called out.

"Think it'll lift?" the plump man asked. "I wanted to try a little fishing."

"Hope so," Ted answered. "Where're you from?"

"Port Jefferson," the skipper told him.

"You're a long way from home." Ted's admiring eyes traveled the boat's length and back. "Meet anybody else out here?"

"Heard another boat a while back but didn't get a look at her." The plump man waved a friendly hand. "Well, guess we'll stick it out a little longer."

Ted waved back, and the motors came to life. As the *Traveler* moved gently off, the two men on the de luxe craft returned to their cabin.

"I suppose it was Anthony they saw," Ted said absent-mindedly, turning his head to watch the sleek boat disappear into the fog. "She sure is a beauty, isn't she?"

"That," Ken said quietly, "was the boat we saw last night."

CHAPTER V

LOBSTERS ABOARD

SANDY AND TED both stared blankly at Ken.

"The boat you saw last night?" Ted repeated unbelievingly.

"You know, I think you're right," Sandy said slowly. He twisted his head to try to get another look at the slim black craft that had already disappeared in the mist. "Did you ever see him before, Ted?" he asked, swinging back.

"No." Ted shook his head. "And come to think of it, not many sport boats go out in weather like this." Ted kept his eyes on the water as the *Traveler* moved ahead, but he looked puzzled. "They usually wait until it clears," he said. "Fishermen like—" He stopped abruptly. "There's one of our traps."

Ken and Sandy followed his pointing finger, and Ken spotted a red and white speck bobbing up and down on the surface.

"Is that it—about a hundred feet ahead and to the left?"

"Portside, you mean, landlubber," Ted corrected him,

swinging the wheel slightly. His body was tensed, and he was again the authoritative skipper.

Both Ken and Sandy realized that there would be no further opportunity for discussion and speculation now.

"Give us our orders," Ken said. "Hey!" he added. "It's clearing right ahead."

Even as he spoke a faint breeze sprang up out of nowhere, and the fog swirled and seemed to divide into segments.

"Good." Ted's voice was brusque. "Get that boat hook, Sandy, and get ready to snag the float as I go by."

"Aye, aye, sir. Take it easy," Sandy added as he stood poised at the rail.

The *Traveler* slowed.

Sandy lunged, and then pulled the hook back, bringing with it the cork buoy and the line to which it was attached. "Got it!"

Ted threw the boat into reverse and stopped it dead. He took the wet line from Sandy's fingers, looped it over the pulley at the end of the boom, and yanked in enough slack to permit the line to reach the drum of the winch. Deftly then he wrapped the line twice around the drum and started the winch. The line came rapidly aboard, the water squeezing out of it as it ran tightly around the drum.

Ken kept his eyes on the water, waiting for the trap itself to appear. "Here it is!"

A wooden-slatted crate, some four feet long, two feet wide and a foot deep, lifted slowly out of the water. Ted stopped the winch when it hung a few yards above the rail. "Swing the boom over the deck," he directed.

When the trap was poised almost amidships, he let the line slip back until the dripping lobster pot thudded onto the deck. All three boys bent over it.

There were no slats at one end of the crate. Instead, there was fish net, stretched taut in the shape of a funnel narrowing down to a small opening inside the crate. Dangling in that opening were the bony skeletons of four bunkers hanging from a loop of twine.

"Something ate the bait, anyway," Sandy pointed out.

"That doesn't mean anything," Ted said. He removed the lid of the crate, and the boys stared at the quantity of rubbery green vegetation inside.

Sandy fingered a piece of it. "Nice haul of seaweed."

"Usually when a trap is full of kelp," Ted said, pulling out more of the green stuff, "there's a lobster or two inside. But if Jackson was out last night . . ."

"There! To the left—isn't that a lobster?" Ken asked.

Ted pulled out the rest of the kelp and disclosed a large bluish-green lobster crawling on the bottom, its antennae and claws aimlessly waving.

"What do you know!" Ted sounded surprised. "Jackson must have overlooked this pot." He grasped the lobster firmly by the body just behind the head and hefted it. "Five pounds."

"Just don't ask me to hold him for you," Sandy said.

Ted grinned. "You've got to know how," he admitted. Keeping the lobster well away from his body, so that the murderous-looking claws couldn't seize his clothes, he took two small wooden pegs from a coffee tin standing beside the compass. Then, clamping the lobster between his knees, he pushed a plug into each claw hinge.

"There. Now he can't open his claws, and can't fight

with the other lobsters—provided we get any more, that is." Ted dropped his catch into one of the tubs of sea water. "If they do get to fighting in there," he explained, "they pull each other's claws off. And a lobster minus a claw isn't worth as much as one with full equipment."

Sandy was removing the loop of fishbones from inside the funnel. "What's this in the bottom of the crate?" he asked. "Concrete?"

"Sure," Ted told him. "To weight the pot down." He fastened in a string of fresh bunkers and replaced the lid of the trap. "O.K. We're ready to put her back."

He got the winch moving once more, lifted the trap off the deck, waited until Sandy had swung the boom out over the side, and then let the rope slip backward until the trap had disappeared under the water, pulling the line with it as it sank. When only a few feet of line remained on deck, Ted threw the buoy overboard.

"That's that," he said, returning to the wheel and starting the *Traveler's* motor again. "Now for the next one—not that I'm expecting to find any more lobsters."

But he was mistaken. The next trap—discovered easily enough, in the rapidly thinning mist—yielded three lobsters, one of which was undersized and had to be thrown back. The third pot was empty, but the fourth held another five-pounder.

As they hauled the tenth pot, and added the seventeenth and eighteenth lobsters to the tub, Ted shook his head.

"Maybe Jackson wasn't around here after all last night," he muttered.

The fifteenth pot was being lowered back over the

side when Ted spotted another boat working a half mile away off their port bow.

Ken sighted it at the same moment. "Who's that?"

"The *Stingray*," Ted said. "Wonder how Anthony's making out."

But they didn't leave the line to inquire, and by noon they had hauled fifty-five pots. Ted estimated that their catch totaled nearly two hundred pounds.

"Let's have lunch," he suggested. "That's a good morning's work—especially for softies that aren't used to it," he added with a grin.

Sandy looked surprised. "You've kept us so busy I haven't even noticed I was hungry. But now that you mention it—" and he dived promptly for the galley.

Before lunch was ready they sighted the *Stingray* again, and this time Ted opened the throttle and headed for her.

While they were still some distance away Anthony raised his arm in a cheerful salute. "Left me alone last night," he called out. "We're doing fine."

"So are we," Ted called back. But when the water between them had dwindled to a narrow channel, he added, "He was out last night, though. Steve says he fueled up when he came in yesterday, and he was fueling again this morning."

Anthony looked perplexed. "That's funny. Wonder who he raided."

"Not Dad's line, I hope."

"I hope not too." Then Anthony gestured to his gawky young helper, and the *Stingray* drew off.

When the last pot had been hauled and rebaited, Ted looked at his watch with amazement. "I'll hire you guys any time," he said. "It's only three thirty and we're finished for the day. That's a long line too."

"And a good catch," Sandy said admiringly, studying the tubs of slowly moving lobsters. "Must be three hundred pounds of them."

"More than that, I'd guess. Well, even if Dad and Hank didn't do much, we can't complain today."

Ted lashed the boom in place and hosed down the deck, sweeping the debris through the scuppers into the sea. Then he fixed the hose so that a constant stream of sea water poured into the tubs.

"O.K.," he said finally. "Now for home." He set a course north by east, opened the throttle full, and motioned the boys to join him on the cabin roof. "Might as well relax," he said, resting his feet on the spokes of the wheel. "I can run her from here until we reach the inlet."

Ken and Sandy stretched out near him, squinting their eyes at the sky that was now a clear blue, and letting the gentle rise and fall of the boat ease their tired muscles. Up ahead of them two other boats were making their way home.

"I wonder," Ken said finally, "what that black boat's doing."

"Fishing," Sandy said, trying to beat a yawn with the word and not quite making it.

"Ted said no," Ken reminded him.

"I said he probably wouldn't be fishing in that fog," Ted countered. "He may *be* a fisherman, for all—" He interrupted himself. "In fact he is. Trolling right now— over there to starboard."

Ken and Sandy sat up.

Ken narrowed his eyes against the glare of the water, and finally made out the black boat cruising along on a course parallel with their own. The tiny figure in the cockpit seemed to be holding a rod.

"Got a pair of glasses?" Ken asked.

Ted nodded. "On one of the bunks, below."

Ken remained in the cabin for several minutes before he reappeared, to speak to them from the deck. "I was looking at them through the window—fortunately."

"What does that mean?" Sandy asked.

"Because the tall one—the skipper—is watching *us* through glasses."

Both Ted and Sandy left the cabin roof to join him. Ted took the glasses, went into the cabin for a minute, and nodded as he came out.

"You're right," he told Ken. "But what's the idea?"

When Sandy returned from the cabin, after his turn with the glasses, he said excitedly, "He's watching all the boats—ours, and those two up ahead, and something behind."

They all turned at his words, and simultaneously recognized the *Stingray* some distance seaward.

"What's more," Sandy went on, "if he's trolling, I'm a flying fish. I saw him reel in and put his rod down—and if he had more than twenty feet of line out, I'll eat it."

There was silence for a long moment as all three of them stared across the wide glittering water toward the small black shape.

It was Ted who finally spoke. "It's not illegal to pretend you're trolling, and to use binoculars. Maybe he's an amateur and doesn't know any better."

"An amateur—with that boat?" Ken raised his eyebrows skeptically. "But I wouldn't be so curious if we hadn't seen him last night," he added.

Ted suddenly took the glasses and looked at a far-off lobster boat they hadn't noticed before. "Dad's coming in, too," he said after a moment. "We'll beat him, though."

"Look at our black friend," Ken said.

The sleek craft was cutting the water rapidly now, its stern out of sight in the foamy wake the screws churned, its bow high. The trolling figure had disappeared.

Ted whistled quietly. "She's really moving."

Before the *Traveler* had gone another two miles, the black boat had rounded the headland marking the entrance to the bay. And by the time Ted changed his course to head westward down the bay toward Eastend, she was out of sight. The next time the boys sighted her she was taking on gasoline at the pump where the boys had fueled that morning.

A few minutes later Ted was easing the *Traveler* alongside her own dock, and the boys made her fast.

Ken kept his eyes on the black boat across the harbor. "Think we'll keep an eye on the dock tonight," he muttered. "Maybe we can see what goes on."

Mr. Bateson whistled when he came ashore from the *Mary Bateson*, some twenty minutes later. "I thought *we* did all right," he said. He turned to Hank. "What have we got?"

"Good two hundred pounds."

"About what I thought. But look what the boys brought in."

Hank shook his head wonderingly. "Did you see Anthony?"

Ted nodded. "He did all right. How about Unger and Smith?"

"Good catches—both of them," his father answered. "But Jackson was certainly out last night. He—"

"We know. Refueled last night and again this morning."

Mr. Bateson scratched the stubble on his chin. "What do you make of it, Hank?"

Hank shrugged. "I say we take these lobsters in and stop wasting time on that—" He swallowed the last word.

"Mind if we tie up at your dock tonight?" The voice calling from beyond the end of the pier startled them all. The sleek black boat stood about twenty feet off the dock, and it was the plump man, smiling pleasantly at them from the rear cockpit, who had spoken. His skipper was at the wheel.

"Why not?" Mr. Bateson started toward them, his voice cordial. "Just so you keep clear of us. We leave pretty early."

"We'll do that," the skipper called. "Thanks."

"If you need some water," Mr. Bateson went on, "use that hose there." He pointed to a coiled rubber hose attached to a faucet at the end of the dock.

"Thanks again." The black boat reversed and then came forward to glide along the dock on the opposite side from the two lobster boats. Ted and Sandy caught the lines and made her fast.

Ken moved to where he could look down at the sharply pointed bow, and then wandered back toward the stern. The word *Dolphin* was painted in small gray letters there, scarcely visible against the black paint.

"My name's Thompson," the plump man said to Mr. Bateson when the engines were stilled. "Jones and I— we're just fooling around trying to catch some fish."

"That's a fast boat for fishing."

Thompson smiled. "I like speed."

"She's mighty pretty." Then Mr. Bateson, with a friendly "Just make yourselves at home," walked back up the dock to Hank. "Well, let's get the lobsters moving."

Ken joined the two men. "That's the boat we saw here last night," he said quietly.

Mr. Bateson, who had started toward the shed to bring out the truck, didn't lose a step. "You're sure?"

"We were pretty sure when we met her outside today," Ken answered. "But now I'm positive. You've painted the end pilings of the dock white."

"Sure." Mr. Bateson looked at him curiously. "See 'em better in the dark that way."

"There's a white streak on that boat's bow—and a black streak on your white paint. They must have misjudged the distance when they pulled in last night."

CHAPTER VI

THE *DOLPHIN* SLIPS OUT

TWENTY MINUTES after the three boys had gone up
stairs with the intention of cleaning up for supper they
were still in their work clothes and still discussing the
Dolphin.

Ted sat on Ken's bed, leaning back against the head
board. "O.K.," he said. "So she was in here last night
But lots of people use our dock. It's close to the inlet
it's pretty good-sized, it's safe, it's got a water supply."

"But wouldn't he have asked permission first?" Sandy
wondered.

Ted shrugged. "You saw the man about half an hour
after our downstairs lights went out. Maybe he'd come
up to the house to ask permission, and then changed
his mind because he didn't want to wake us up."

"Then why did he take off right afterward?" Ken
began to unbutton his shirt.

"Because he didn't get permission." Ted stood up
"I'd better dress too. Dad'll be back in a couple of min
utes, and Mom's broiling lobsters for supper."

Sandy unzipped his shirt with one gesture. "Why didn't you say so earlier?"

Ted paused at the door to grin back over his shoulder. "Didn't want to interrupt detectives at work," he said. "So I also didn't mention there'll be New England clam chowder first."

Sandy picked up his towel when the door had closed behind Ted. "I bet he thinks we let our imagination run away with us," he said. "Maybe we do." He looked at Ken and then shrugged elaborately. "Since the mastermind seems completely lost in thought, I'll take first crack at the bathroom."

But when Sandy returned five minutes later, Ken was still staring out the window toward the *Dolphin*.

"Hey," Sandy said. He got a fresh shirt out of the bureau and put it on, and ran a hand over his already water-slicked hair. "Hey!" he repeated then. "Come to, will you? Mr. Bateson's home."

Ken walked absently across the room toward the door. "Too many questions without answers," he muttered, with one hand on the knob. "If Jackson used up a tank of fuel last night, what was he doing—if not robbing lobster pots? Why was the *Dolphin's* skipper watching the lobster boats so carefully? Why was the plump one—Thompson—pretending to be trolling?" He started out the door, came back to grab up his towel from the rack, and headed for the door again. "And how long has Jackson been pirating lobsters, anyway?" he added before he disappeared.

An hour later Mrs. Bateson was looking with amazement at the heap of clean lobster shells on Sandy's plate.

"Sandy," she said with a smile, "you're the best tonic

for a tired housewife I ever saw. Just to see you eat makes me want to go right out to the kitchen and cook another whole meal."

"Mom!" Ted sounded hurt. "*I* always eat everything you cook."

His mother shook her head. "You're not even in Sandy's class, Ted."

"Well, he'll be sorry," Ted said with mock resentment, "when he sees your deep-dish apple pie—and can't eat a mouthful."

"I wouldn't count on that," Ken warned Ted.

Sandy ate two pieces of the pie, though he agreed to the second one only after the boys had announced that they would do the dishes, so that Mr. and Mrs. Bateson could leave early to visit friends down the coast.

"Oh, well," Sandy had said then, resignedly, helping himself to the last wedge on the plate. "I could do without this," he explained, "but I don't want you to think we're too lazy to wash an extra dish."

Mrs. Bateson was still smiling when she and her husband left.

A knock on the back door came just as Ted was drying off the drainboard. "Come in," he called.

The plump Mr. Thompson stood in the doorway, and behind him loomed the tall, thin skipper.

"Sorry to bother you," Thompson said, "but Jones and I decided not to eat on board tonight. We wondered if you could recommend a good restaurant somewhere near by—within walking distance, that is."

Ted hung up the dishcloth and moved to the door. "There's a diner in town—only about fifteen minutes from here."

"Good." Thompson beamed. "Which way?"

"Right on our street, across the square from the wholesale fish company. You can't miss it."

"Thanks—thanks very much."

When the door had closed on them, Ken left the kitchen on a run. Ted and Sandy stared at each other. The front door clicked open and Sandy shook his head. "Don't mind him," he said. "He's convinced those two are up to no good."

Ken returned as abruptly as he had left. "I guess they're really heading for the diner all right," he said.

Ted leaned against the sink and laughed. "What did you expect them to do?"

Ken smiled finally. "I know. Melodrama Holt, they call me. But I think they're interested in something besides fish. And I still want answers to my questions."

"What questions?" Ted asked more seriously. "Maybe I know some answers."

"Well, let's see if you do." Ken sat astride a kitchen chair, facing Ted. "Here goes. What was Jackson doing to use up his fuel last night?"

Ted spoke slowly. "Not robbing lobster pots—we know that. Maybe he just went out for a ride." He shook his head. "No—I give up."

"Two: Why was Jones keeping binoculars on the lobster fleet this afternoon," Ken went on, "and why was Thompson doing that phony trolling? Three: How long has Jackson been pirating your lobsters? How long has he been around here? Is he a native?"

Ted opened his mouth, shut it again, and looked helplessly at Sandy. "Does he always go on like this?"

"Not always," Sandy admitted. "But when he does I

find it's easiest in the long run to humor him." But Sandy's own voice had a note of seriousness in it. He knew his dark-haired friend too well to laugh off one of Ken's typical question periods.

"Well," Ted said slowly, "I can't even guess about the *Dolphin*—but Thompson and his skipper both seemed mighty pleasant just now."

"We've been fooled before by people who seemed pleasant," Sandy told him. "And the trolling *was* phony —I'm sure of that."

Ken flashed him a brief grin and then looked back at Ted.

"I can tell you something about Jackson," Ted went on. "He's new here—came about a year and a half ago from somewhere over on the north shore of the island. This summer is the first time we've suspected him of robbing our pots. Dad and some of the others checked up on him, when we first began to wonder, and they found he had a pretty bad reputation on the north shore too."

"Could they have made it too hot for him over there?" Ken asked.

Ted shrugged. "They apparently did about what we do. The wholesalers stopped buying his lobsters, and he didn't have any friends. There wasn't much else they *could* do."

"Does Jackson own his own place here?"

Ted looked blank. "I don't know. He and his partner —a fellow named Plauk—live together in a little house that had been vacant several years. City people once used it for a summer cottage. Seems to me Dad said it was owned by a bank—a New York bank—because of a mortgage or something. But I don't really know. Since nobody around here talks to Jackson, we don't know much about his affairs."

"When did Anthony come out here? Was that about a year and a half ago too?" Ken asked.

Ted stared at him. "You're not trying to tie those two up together, are you?" he demanded. "You saw last night how Anthony is—it's all Dad can do to keep him from taking a shot at Jackson." He stopped and swallowed. "As a matter of fact," he said then, "Anthony did come out here only a month or so before Jackson —but they've got nothing to do with each other."

"O.K." Ken stood up abruptly. "Let's try a new tack. The *Dolphin's* deserted right now. How about taking a look?"

Ted sank on a chair with a gesture of exaggerated defeat. "I give up. The *Dolphin* must have cost at least fifty thousand dollars. If Thompson had stolen all the lobsters in Eastend for a year, he couldn't have paid for it. So what makes you think—?"

"I don't think anything—yet," Ken assured him with a grin. "But we all agree there's something peculiar about that boat. Thompson probably has nothing to do with Jackson, but I'd like to look the *Dolphin* over just on general principles."

Ted considered. "Dad wouldn't like people to think he lets them use our dock just so they can be spied on."

"I know," Ken said quickly. "But we'll be careful. Suppose you stay here. If they come down the driveway on their way to the dock, you put the kitchen light on. That'll be the signal for us to make ourselves scarce."

Ted agreed, still somewhat reluctant, and turned out

the kitchen light as Ken and Sandy started down the drive. They stopped at the shed to get a flashlight out of the convertible, and waited quietly beside the *Dolphin* a moment to make certain no one was aboard. Then they dropped softly into the rear cockpit and moved forward to the cabin door.

Ken tried the knob. "Locked."

"There's another door." Sandy padded on his sneakers along the narrow catwalk that skirted the cabin and dropped noiselessly onto the soft leather upholstery of the seat in the front cockpit. A moment later he returned. "It's locked too."

"Let's see what we can see through the window."

They leaned close, directed the flashlight's beam through the glass, and shaded it with their hands.

The interior of the cabin was as luxurious as the sleek lines of the boat promised it would be. Heavy overstuffed leather benches ran along the wall, and the lower half of the bulkhead was mahogany polished to a fine luster. Beyond the bulkhead a narrow companionway ran forward, and they could dimly make out doors opening off it on either side. But the cabin itself was neat and uninformative.

After a moment the boys climbed the two steps that led to the catwalk and looked through the forward windows. The first small sleeping cabin was bare—even the bunks were unmade. The room ahead of that on the starboard side was a bathroom, and forward of that was another stateroom—this one apparently being used. Folded newspapers lay on a desk just inside the window. Ahead was the engine room, its metal shining with cleanliness.

"The other side?" Sandy asked.

They crossed over the cabin roof and dropped onto the port deck. There the forward stateroom disclosed a shirt and a pair of trousers lying limply on a chair. The second stateroom, like its twin across the corridor, seemed unused.

Ken flicked off the light. "There wasn't anything on that starboard cabin desk except a newspaper, was there?" he murmured after a moment of thought. And then he added, "Let's check again."

But the back of the desk was against the window, and if there were papers in the pigeonholes they were invisible from where the boys stood. Ken maneuvered the flashlight's beam back and forth, and then held it fixedly on the newspaper. A heavy pencil mark circled a small area.

"If we had the binoculars . . ."

"I'll get 'em from the car," Sandy said quickly.

When he returned he handed them to Ken, took the flashlight, and held it steady.

Ken focused on the modest heading of the marked column, and spelled out the upside-down letters. "Incoming ships. Due today."

"What day?" Sandy asked, and moved the light toward the upper edge of the paper.

"Today," Ken said, reading the date. "All right. Let's try it." The light moved back to the pencil mark again and Ken braced his arm against the window frame to hold the glasses rigid. Letter by letter he read the small type. "The *Northbird* . . . sailing from Rotterdam."

"What do you suppose—?" Sandy began, and then broke off suddenly and doused the light.

Instinctively they both turned their heads toward the kitchen windows. But the whole back of the Bateson house was dark.

Then they heard it again—a faint creak and a small rattle.

Ken identified it. "Oarlocks," he whispered.

They climbed silently up on the dock and moved forward to huddle behind a stack of lobster pots. To their straining ears the small sounds grew louder, and soon they could follow the progress of the still-invisible boat being rowed around the end of the dock toward the side where the *Dolphin* lay.

There was a gentle scraping noise. And then, through the slats of the lobster pots, they saw a thin beam of light flash up over the far side of the *Dolphin's* rear cockpit. The light moved forward along the boat's deck, lifted, and suddenly reflected backward from the glass of the cabin doorway, dimly revealing Jackson's bulking long-armed figure.

Ken stiffened, and felt Sandy go rigid beside him.

Jackson tried the door, turned off his light as he moved stealthily across the cabin roof, and turned it on again as he tried the front cockpit entrance.

Ken's head swung swiftly. Out of the corner of his eye he had seen vivid yellow rectangles bloom against darkness. The light was on in the Bateson kitchen.

He looked back just in time to catch the dim shape of Jackson's figure, scurrying without the aid of a flashlight now, to the *Dolphin's* rear cockpit. An instant later oarlocks rattled again. The rowboat was heading out into the harbor.

With his hand on Sandy's arm, to draw him along,

Ken led the way to the deck of the *Mary Bateson*, where they waited in silence.

Jones and Thompson appeared very shortly, strolling leisurely in the path of the powerful flash the skipper carried.

"Nice night," Thompson said.

"Fine."

Neither of them spoke again. Thompson unlocked the *Dolphin's* cabin door, they both entered, and the door shut behind them. The cabin lights came on and then disappeared almost immediately as the curtains were drawn over the small windows.

Ted was waiting at the shed by the time Ken and Sandy's cautious retreat had reached that point.

"Did they see you?" Ted asked quietly.

Ken shook his head reassuringly. Inside the shelter of the shed he told Ted about their fruitless visit to the *Dolphin*—fruitless except for the marked name of a ship in a newspaper column—and then reported Jackson's furtive visit to the handsome craft.

"It doesn't make any sense to me—any of it," Ted said finally. "Maybe Dad—" He stopped. "Listen!"

It was several seconds before Ken and Sandy could catch the faint sound Ted's more experienced ear had heard—the muted throb of an overhead exhaust. Even when they stood beside Ted in the dark shed doorway a full minute went by before they could chart the course of a boat moving without lights through the harbor toward the inlet.

Ted took a step through the doorway, and then froze. Another sound reached them. This time it was a quiet gurgle and the swish of water.

Ted moved forward again then, very cautiously, and the boys followed. The gurgle grew fainter as they approached the dock, but even as they set careful foot on the wooden planking they caught the strong smell of exhaust fumes.

Ted broke into a run.

Water was still swirling in disturbed patterns around the pilings of the dock, but otherwise no sign of the *Dolphin* remained. She had slipped her moorings and vanished.

Three pairs of eyes turned simultaneously to focus on the blinking harbor light, and once again their ears picked up the dull beat of the overhead exhaust. And then that beat died, and silence lay heavy over the harbor.

"Could they both be outside so fast?" Ken asked.

"Not without passing in front of the blinker. The tide's going out," Ted added. "They're probably drifting with it."

"There!" Ken said.

The silhouette of a boat blacked out two flashes of the inlet light—a lobster boat, her mast and boom clearly outlined in each of the momentary glows.

"Jackson?" Sandy asked.

"Probably." Ted's voice was grim. "Though all lobster boats look pretty much alike, so I couldn't swear to it."

But no one questioned the next shape that, a moment or two later, again obscured the harbor light. All of them recognized immediately the slim low outline of the *Dolphin*, moving out through the inlet on the silent tide.

CHAPTER VII

FLASH IN THE NIGHT

"I'LL TELL YOU one thing," Ted said, after a minute of thought, "Jones knows these waters pretty well or he wouldn't take a chance on letting the tide carry him through the inlet."

"Why not?" Sandy asked. "All he'd have to do is drift with the current."

Ted shook his head. "The current'll take you right across the bar. And the *Dolphin* draws at least four feet —which is one foot too much. He'd be stuck." He turned back toward the house and the boys turned with him. "No—the *Dolphin* would have to go through the channel, and that would mean tricky steering with only the tide for motive power."

"I wish your father were home," Ken said shortly.

Just then headlights swung into the driveway from the street.

"There he comes," Ted said in surprise.

The car stopped at the house, where Mrs. Bateson got out, and then continued to the shed where the boys awaited it.

"We're back early," Mr. Bateson explained, when he stepped out of the car and joined them. "Hal wasn't feeling very well, so we didn't stay. He—" He broke off to peer at the three sober faces. "What's up?"

"A lobster boat just sneaked out of the harbor riding the tide, and the *Dolphin* took off after it," Ted said.

"Hmm." Mr. Bateson's face sobered too. "Jackson?"

"Couldn't tell for sure, Dad. But it probably was."

"Couldn't we go after them and see what's up?" Ken asked suddenly.

"Well—" The lobsterman rubbed his chin. "Ordinarily I'd say it would be useless." He thought a moment. "If we assume Jackson knows what lines we worked today, we can guess he won't go there—wouldn't be worth his while. He'd be heading for the lines we baited yesterday and the day before."

"That's our number two on the west run, Dad," Ted said eagerly, "and Anthony's number one is out there too. And on the east run it's our number four. Unger's got a line out that way. Couldn't we—?"

"Probably a waste of gas," Mr. Bateson muttered. "But if we got hold of Anthony—and got Unger and Smith out too—well, we might give him a scare, anyway."

"Say!" Sandy looked excited. "Could the *Dolphin* be a Coast Guard boat working undercover to—" His voice died as he saw Mr. Bateson shaking his head.

"Coast Guard doesn't work undercover, son. Ordinarily, that is," he added as he saw Sandy's crestfallen expression. Then he started briskly for the house. "Let's get on the phone."

Five minutes later Mr. Bateson set the receiver back

on the hook for the last time. "Smith and Unger are leaving immediately. No answer at Anthony's house."

"Try the diner," Ted suggested. "He often eats there and hangs around afterward playing shuffleboard."

But the proprietor of the diner said that Anthony had come and gone an hour earlier.

Mr. Bateson stood up. "Well, we won't waste any more time—we'll go out with four boats. I'll go change."

"I'll take a quick run over to Anthony's house," Ted said. "If he's in his shed he might not have heard the phone bell."

"Good idea." His father smiled briefly. "He's been after us for so long to do this—he'd be sore as a boil if he didn't get in on it."

Mr. Bateson and the boys were back downstairs, dressed in their work clothes, when Ted returned.

"He's not there, Dad—and the *Stingray's* gone!"

"That's not so good." Mr. Bateson's forehead wrinkled in concern. "He's such a hothead. If he's out ahead of us, on his own—"

The kitchen door opened and Hank Bower came in. "This is a fool business," he said with his usual abruptness. "How much start has he got?"

"About twenty minutes."

"Well, let's be on our way then."

Mr. Bateson issued brief orders. Ted and the boys would take the *Traveler* out to the number two line, and would swing around Anthony's line there too. The *Mary Bateson,* together with Smith's and Unger's boats, would try to cover the big stretch of water on the east.

"But be careful," was his last word at the dock. "And if you run across Anthony, tell him to keep his shirt on."

The *Mary Bateson* went out first, the tiny red light on her portside, the green one to starboard, and the white light on the mast pricking bright holes in the darkness. The *Traveler* followed.

"But our running lights will warn him, won't they?" Ken asked.

Ted nodded, his face grim in the faint glow cast upward from the compass under his hand. "That's why we'll never get close enough to catch him at anything. He'll see us and make sure nothing incriminating is on board. But it's dangerous—*and* illegal—to run without lights."

When the boat began to rise and fall with the bay swell, they could still see the *Mary Bateson's* white light ahead and, farther away, the tiny mast lights signaling the position of Smith's and Unger's boats.

Ken, huddled behind the glass windshield out of the chilly night wind, said thoughtfully after a while, "No wonder Anthony gets so mad. All Jackson has to do is throw a pirated trap overboard—if anyone comes close to him—and there's no evidence of theft. Right?"

"Right," Ted agreed. "That's why we never tried this before."

"But maybe tonight will be different." There was a smug note in Sandy's voice, and when the other two glanced at him he held up the camera case, which neither of them had noticed before. "I've got a concentrated flash reflector here that'll carry five hundred feet. Who knows? We might catch him before he's ready for company." Sandy grinned triumphantly. "I'll go below now and get it ready," and he disappeared into the cabin.

Ted looked questioningly at Ken. "Is he right?"

Ken smiled reminiscently. "And how! He did that out in Colorado—and you never saw such surprised people in your life."

Beyond the first channel marker Ted shifted course, and soon the other three boats were no longer visible. At the next marker, some fifteen minutes farther on, he shifted slightly once more and the *Traveler's* roll changed to a head-on rise and fall. The wind was at their backs now and kicking up a good swell. Each time the *Traveler* lifted her bow to ride over, it hung there for what seemed like long seconds before she dove down into the trough. Spray dashed against the windshield.

"I don't like this," Ted muttered, flicking on the windshield wiper and trying to peer through the blur of water. "At the speed we're going we could ride right over Jackson—he certainly wouldn't put his own lights on until somebody came right at him. Get out the chart, will you?" he asked Ken.

Ken unrolled it and tried to spread it out on the small shelf over the wheel.

"I only need the middle section. Fold it up." Ted laid a flat steel ruler across the chart to hold it in place. "If Jackson's near our number two line, it'll take us an hour to reach there."

For another fifteen minutes they ran along in silence. Ted kept the small compass light off most of the time, switching it on only occasionally to check their position on the chart, and then blacking it out again to give them better visibility.

It was Sandy, long back on deck after preparing his

camera, who finally broke the tense watchful silence.

"Light!" he said suddenly. "Behind us to the left!"

Ted's head swiveled rapidly. "That's ten miles out," he said a moment later. "Ocean liner, probably. Keep an eye on her—you'll see."

A few minutes later the single point of light had multiplied into many evenly spaced ones, as the liner came over the curve of the earth and into full view. She was a long way out and overtaking them fast, her course roughly parallel to their own.

"Heading for New York," Ted explained as the boys watched the distant toylike progress. "Probably due in by daylight. Looks nice, doesn't it?"

"Swell." Ken let his thoughts drift to some future day when he and Sandy might be able to persuade Richard Holt to take them to Europe on one of his news-gathering jaunts. He was in the middle of a delightful daydream involving the head of the French Sûreté—who was asking the help of the "two so-young but so-brilliant American detectives"—when Ted suddenly pushed the throttle to low speed. An instant later the engine was completely shut off, and only the rise and fall of water and the creak of the boom disturbed the quiet.

"Ought to be pretty close now," Ted said quietly.

"Already?" Immediately the thought of Jackson drove from Ken's mind the imaginary criminal that had been occupying it.

"All we can do now is listen for the sound of an engine," Ted explained.

For long minutes they let the *Traveler* wallow and roll at the mercy of the wind and the swells. The ocean liner had passed them, still at her distance, and disappeared over the horizon again. The *Traveler* seemed entirely alone in the vast Atlantic. And the sea was as silent as it was dark. The boys talked occasionally, in brief whispers, but mostly they concentrated all their energies on listening.

"Well," Ted said finally, after an especially long silence, "guess he's not around. Should have heard him by now if he were either at our line or Anthony's." He blinked on the compass light momentarily to look at the clock. "Been here almost an hour. Might as well give up."

"Maybe he saw us coming, and is just floating around himself—waiting for us to leave," Ken suggested.

"Could be," Ted agreed. "But there's a fog coming up and I don't like—" He stopped suddenly.

As the *Traveler* lifted on a wave, Ken and Sandy both heard what had caught Ted's attention—the faint throbbing sound of an exhaust, far away.

It was off their stern, but how far off not even Ted could tell, as the sound swelled and died with the wind. And there was no sign of a light.

"Couldn't you turn our lights off for just a minute?" Sandy suggested. "Otherwise, he'll see us and—"

"Risky business," Ted said firmly.

They all listened intently once more, and simultaneously realized that the throbbing had stopped.

"Guess you were right, Sandy," Ted said grimly. "And he's probably laughing his head off right now because we do obey the law. Now he'll just pick up a lobster buoy and go right ahead."

"Can he find them in the dark?" Ken asked.

"He'll use his searchlight. What's he got to be afraid of?"

"Plenty," Sandy said, cradling his camera securely in his arm. "Just let him show a light—and he'll see."

Suddenly the throbbing started once more, closer this time, but still some distance away. And then a searchlight stabbed through the darkness for a brief instant, sweeping quickly over the water before it vanished.

"I told you," Ted said. "That's the *Sea Robin* or I'll—"

"Head that way," Sandy urged. "If he's not going to worry until we're right on top of him . . ."

The light cut the blackness once more, just as Ted started the engine. "Half a mile," Ted estimated.

Then he headed the *Traveler* around to face the spot where the flash had showed, and opened the throttle halfway. A minute later he shut it off and they listened. The other boat's engine was still running. Ted started the *Traveler* again and moved closer. When he killed his engine this time, the other exhaust was louder than ever.

"Quarter of a mile," Ted said.

"Have to do better than that," Sandy told him.

"Right." There was a new excitement in Ted's voice— a reflection of Sandy's eager hopefulness. He kicked the gears into mesh and the *Traveler* jumped forward.

Two minutes later he shut the power off once more. The sound they all heard had changed slightly.

"He's using the winch," Ted whispered. "Must be hauling up a pot. I'm afraid to get closer—he'll drop it overboard. Do you think—?"

"I'll try it." Sandy climbed up on the cabin roof, bracing himself by wrapping an arm around the mast.

Ken, similarly braced, used his free hand to hold Sandy steady.

"Here goes," Sandy breathed.

As he pressed the release a brilliant beam of light cut through the darkness to pin-point a lobster boat less than two hundred yards off their bow. On its aft deck two men were clearly visible, bent low over what appeared to be a lobster pot.

Almost simultaneously with the flash, Ted turned the *Traveler's* searchlight on and swung it around to bathe the other boat in its glare. The two men had straightened and for an instant stood looking directly into the blaze of light. One of them was unmistakably Jackson.

An instant later the second man—Jackson's partner, Ken and Sandy presumed—dropped flat on the deck, and Jackson himself leaped for the wheelhouse. And then the *Sea Robin's* searchlight flared, pivoted, found the *Traveler*, and shone full in the boys' blinded eyes.

Across the intervening space Jackson's voice roared. "Can't a man look at his own lobster pots without a lot of snoops following him around?"

In the brief silence that followed the boys clearly heard a loud splash.

"There goes the pot," Ted said quietly.

"And if he knows we took a picture," Ken said, just as quietly, "he'll want to get his hand on the camera."

But Jackson apparently had not realized the significance of that first flash. He flicked off his own searchlight and stood boldly in the beam of the *Traveler's*, his big hands on his hips.

"You better go on home, sonny," he shouted. "Fog coming up. Little boys might get lost."

He was laughing as he turned to the *Sea Robin's* controls, to send her plowing through the water on a homeward course that would take her wide around the *Traveler*.

Sandy hugged his camera. "Maybe he won't laugh so hard tomorrow."

Ted smiled wryly. "Hope you're right, but . . ." He kept the *Sea Robin* in the searchlight's beam until it disappeared behind the wisps of fog that were rapidly becoming more frequent. "Guess he's going home all right," he said finally, turning the light off and punching the starter button. A few minutes later the *Traveler* had swung around and was heading shoreward under full throttle.

For half an hour they ran steadily, and entirely by compass.

"If we could see where we're going," Ted muttered, peering vainly through the now-heavy mist, "I'd begin to shift course here. But there's some nasty rocks around the headland, so I've got to give it a wide berth."

"What about the other boats?" Sandy wondered. "Do you suppose we'll meet them on the way in?"

"Very possible. And that doesn't make me feel any safer in this pea soup." Ted pressed the signal button and let the horn roar out its hoarse warning. There was no answering blast, but he pressed it again a moment later.

As if in protest to the noise, the *Traveler's* engine coughed and missed several beats. It caught again immediately, ran smoothly for a moment, and then sputtered once more. This time it didn't recover.

The sudden silence was startling.

Ted, looking more amazed than worried, pressed the starter button and let the electric motor spin the engine for a long ten seconds. There was no response.

"I'd better stop that," he said slowly. "Runs the batteries down."

"Out of gas?" Sandy suggested, his voice level.

Ted looked at the gasoline gauge, tapping it to make sure it was in operating order. The needle, which had been over the quarter-full mark, suddenly dropped back to zero and remained there.

Ted turned to look at Ken and Sandy. "Yes," he said flatly. "Out of gas."

"The horn?" Ken suggested, after a moment.

Ted shrugged. "In this fog? Even if anybody's around, they'd just think we were signaling for safety's sake—and keep out of our way." He bent over the chart. "If I'm right about our position," he said, half to himself, "there's about a hundred and fifty feet of water under us now. That's a long way down for our anchor to hold."

"Why anchor?" Sandy asked. "Can't we just drift around until daylight—and somebody comes to find us?"

"Tide will be coming in soon. Unless we can hold fast, it will pile us up on the beach. Or," Ted added grimly, "on those rocks I was just talking about."

CHAPTER VIII

STRANGE DEVELOPMENT

As TED PUNCHED the signal button once more, the sound brayed out into the fog. There was no answering signal. Then he switched the searchlight on, but now it penetrated no more than fifty feet, and the glare thrown back by the mist blinded them. He cut it off.

"Look," Ted said, "don't get me wrong about this. We're in no real danger. Even if the anchor drags a bit, she'll probably take hold when we get in shallower water—long before we hit the beach or the rocks. Dad'll worry if we don't get back, but that can't be helped. So let's throw the anchor over and see what happens."

"Sure." Ken's voice echoed the calm note that Ted had managed to get into his own. The three boys started to climb on the cabin roof to walk forward to where the anchor was lashed to blocks on the deck.

But as Ted hoisted himself up, a boat horn suddenly blared behind them.

Ted was back at the controls and sending out his answer before the first sound had died.

"Your father?" Ken asked.

Ted shook his head and gestured for silence as the

strange horn blared once more and the *Traveler* answered again. A moment later, not far astern, a glow appeared in the mist—a powerful searchlight trying to fight the fog.

Ted flipped his own light switch and pressed the signal button in one motion. He swiveled his searchlight around, blinked it off and on. The hazy glow behind them disappeared and reappeared too, and the other boat's horn blared.

Ted tipped his light down until it illuminated the aft deck. Then, standing in the full glare, he waved.

"Ahoy!" The voice sounded very close. "Who's there?"

Ted shouted through the megaphone of his cupped hands. "The *Traveler!* We're out of gas!"

"Stand by!"

Slowly the boys could make out the dim shape of an approaching craft—could even distinguish a figure silhouetted by the searchlight.

"The *Dolphin!*" Ken exclaimed.

"Your light's blinding us!" the voice from the *Dolphin* called.

Sandy flipped off the switch and left the *Traveler* bathed in the other boat's beam. Now they could hear the muffled gurgle of the twin underwater exhausts as the black craft inched up to their stern. Twenty feet away it went into reverse, stopped dead, and rolled heavily to the swells.

It was Thompson who had been hailing them. Now he came forward and dropped into the cockpit to lean over his bow. "What's going on out here tonight?" he asked. "A regatta?"

Ted ignored the question. "Got any gas to spare?"

"Sure." Thompson didn't press his query. "But how do we get it to you? This swell—"

His skipper broke in. "Be easier if we tow you in. Throw us a line."

"O.K." Ted turned his searchlight on again and illuminated his own cabin roof. Then he climbed forward, carrying a coil of one-inch line.

While the *Dolphin* eased herself past, keeping twenty feet away, Ted made the end of the line fast to the *Traveler's* bow. When it was secure he picked up the coil of line and threw it across the intervening space. Thompson, in the aft cockpit, caught it neatly.

"How much line have you got?" he called, bending down to fasten his end to a bitt on the *Dolphin's* stern.

"About seventy feet," Ted called back. "Ought to do."

"Sure." The *Dolphin* began to draw slowly ahead. "When we get inside the bay we'll be able to pull alongside and give you some gas. You'll dock easier under your own power." He waved as the *Dolphin* began to disappear into the fog.

Ted turned off the searchlight and an instant later the *Traveler* lurched gently as the line stretched taut. Slowly her bow swung to follow the hawser, and the helpless roll of the boat changed to a forward motion as she got under way. Up ahead the *Dolphin's* light had been turned to face them, and Ted's firm hands on the wheel kept the *Traveler* headed directly at the blob of light.

"Happy coincidence," Ken muttered.

"Coincidence?" Sandy repeated. "You know we don't like coincidences."

"Happy, anyway." The relief in Ted's voice was a

measure of how worried he had been. "And let me tell you something else," he added a moment later. "That man Thompson is no amateur sailor. Did you see how he caught that line and made it fast?"

Sandy looked over the side at the swirling water. "And that boat's no toy, either," he commented. "She's pulling us almost as fast as we can go by ourselves."

Ted whistled quietly, his eye on the compass. "He's cutting it close. Either he's taking an awful chance in this fog, or he's got X-ray eyes."

"Radar, maybe," Ken suggested.

Ted snorted. "Not even fancy jobs like that have radar equipment ordinarily."

"Not many have engines like the *Dolphin's,* either," Ken pointed out.

Up ahead the searchlight veered slightly to port and Ted moved the wheel to follow. "We're going around the headland. Keep your fingers crossed."

The light swung still further to port and again Ted pulled the *Traveler's* bow over. The line remained taut —the boat ahead of them maintained its steady pace.

Ted's hands clenched on the mahogany spokes of his wheel as he brought it still further over. Then for fifteen minutes they kept a straight course, until the light ahead swung suddenly to starboard. Ted swung the wheel hard to keep up, and then reversed just as rapidly as the *Dolphin* veered to port.

Almost immediately the channel marker appeared ahead, its red light flashing on and off. A moment later it had vanished in the mist off their stern, and simultaneously the swells diminished and the *Traveler* stopped heaving.

The perspiration on Ted's face glistened in the light from the binnacle as he took one hand off the wheel to mop his forehead. "Brother!" he said hoarsely. "That's what I call navigation—or just plain insanity!"

The cable slackened and they could feel the *Traveler* slow down. From ahead came a hail.

"Ahoy, *Traveler!* We're coming back! Take up the slack."

Ted left the wheel and hurried forward. "Light me up," he said over his shoulder.

Sandy switched on the searchlight and Ted began to haul at the line and coil it on deck as the *Dolphin* reversed. Her squat stern came into view, coming back slowly through water churned to foam by the twin screws. Thompson had untied the line, and when the boats were only several yards apart he threw it across. A few moments later Jones's skillful maneuvering brought the *Dolphin's* rope bumpers up against the *Traveler's* side.

Thompson had disappeared into the cabin, and now he emerged with a five-gallon can which he handed across to Sandy. "We'll stand by," he said, "until you get your engine going."

The motor caught at once when Ted spun the starter.

"O.K.?" the plump man asked as Sandy handed back the empty tin.

"O.K." Ted assured him. "And thanks. We'll see you at the dock—and we'll return the gas."

Thompson smiled. "We owe you at least that much for the use of the dock. Forget it."

Ted checked his compass and got the *Traveler* moving, keeping an eye on the searchlight ahead. But now the *Dolphin* had reduced her speed, and she remained a steady seventy-five feet ahead of them all the way, picking up the channel markers with unerring accuracy and going through the inlet into Eastend harbor as steadily as a cat walks a fence.

Mr. Bateson had lighted the floodlight on the end of the dock, and by its light they made fast—the *Traveler* on one side, at the *Mary Bateson's* stern, the *Dolphin* on the other.

"What kept you so long?" Mr. Bateson asked, coming close. "Catch any sight of our friend?"

Ted nodded and then, seeing Thompson and Jones approach, said, "We ran out of gas, Dad. The *Dolphin* towed us into the bay and then gave us five gallons."

"Lucky the *Dolphin* was out there," a new voice commented, and Anthony materialized out of the shadows. "Kind of a rough night for fishing, wasn't it?" he asked Thompson.

"We weren't fishing." Thompson's smile was easy. "We saw boats leaving, so we just thought we'd follow and see what was up." He turned to Mr. Bateson. "What *was* going on? You don't usually go out at night, do you?"

"No, we don't." It was Anthony who answered. "But there's someone here who likes our lobsters so well that he does go out at night to pirate our traps."

"Where were you, Mr. Anthony," Ted began, "when we—?"

"He was already out, Ted," his father broke in. "He saw our friend slipping out and decided to follow."

"He turned eastward when he passed the headland." Anthony sounded disgusted. "I lost him after that."

"No wonder," Ted told him. "He swung way around. We found him over by our number two string with a pot aboard."

"See the marker?" Anthony asked excitedly.

"You know they could never get close enough for that," Mr. Bateson said.

"But we may have got some evidence, Dad."

There was a moment's startled silence.

"Evidence? What do you mean?" Anthony stepped forward.

"Sandy has some kind of a long-distance gadget on his camera," Ted explained. "He took a picture before Jackson threw the pot back. If it comes out . . ." He shrugged.

"We'll get it developed tomorrow," Sandy explained, "and see what we have—if anything. He was pretty far off."

"Why wait until tomorrow? What about tonight?" Anthony suggested.

"I don't have any developing equipment with me."

"But I've got a darkroom," Anthony told him eagerly. "Photography has been a hobby of mine for years. Give me the roll. I'll put it through right now."

Sandy hesitated. "Well—I like to do my own stuff. But if you wouldn't mind letting me borrow—"

"Sure." Anthony smiled. "I know how you feel. I'm the same way. Come on over to my house," he added, turning to include Mr. Bateson and the other boys in his invitation, "and let's see what he's got."

"Would you mind if we came along?" Thompson's voice was diffident. "I know this is all none of our business, but you've got us curious too."

Ken looked at Mr. Bateson. Would the lobsterman remember that the *Dolphin* had followed *one* boat out —not "boats," as Thompson had just said? But even as he momentarily met Mr. Bateson's puzzled eyes, he knew that the *Dolphin's* rescue of the *Traveler* had earned both Thompson and Jones the right to courtesy —at least in Ted's father's opinion.

"Well—" Mr. Bateson began.

"Why not?" Anthony broke in briskly. "Let's go."

As they all walked the short distance to his house, Anthony was explaining to Sandy that he had been an amateur photographer for many years. And when he showed them all into the cellar, pleasantly fitted up as a game room, he gestured toward the door to his darkroom.

"I'll just duck in there a minute first," Anthony said to Sandy. "Want to make sure I didn't leave some printing paper uncovered. The rest of you make yourselves at home."

A few minutes later the door opened again and Anthony emerged, leaving it ajar behind him this time and the light in the darkroom on. "Lucky I checked," he told Sandy, showing him the box in his hand. "This was open—would have been ruined if I'd put the light on. O.K. now."

The others came to stand in the doorway as he showed Sandy the location of the items he would want to use.

"Pretty nice," Sandy murmured, admiring the neatly arranged equipment. "That's the same kind of developing tank I use. Have you got any fine-grain developer?"

Anthony took down two identical quart bottles from

a shelf over the sink. One was marked DEVELOPER, the other HYPO. "Both fresh," he reassured Sandy, removing the lids.

"Looks mighty complicated," Mr. Bateson murmured, glancing at the big enlarger. Thompson and Jones, too, seemed impressed as they examined a delicate scale and studied a long row of bottles.

Idly Thompson picked up a small container. "Photography certainly requires a lot of equipment."

"Take it easy with that bottle," Anthony told him hastily. "That's cyanide—poison."

"Oh!" Thompson almost dropped it in his hurry to put it back on the shelf.

"You stay in here with me—will you, Ken?" Sandy asked. "I may need a hand with this film cartridge—it sticks sometimes."

"Sure."

When Anthony had herded the others out, and shut the darkroom door, Ken flipped off the light switch to obtain the darkness he knew Sandy would require.

"Hold it a minute, Ken." Sandy's voice was scarcely above a whisper. "Turn the light back on."

Ken obeyed. "What—?"

Quickly Sandy aimed his camera at the light bulb, pressed the release, wound the film, and made another exposure with the camera in the same position.

"What are you doing?" Ken demanded.

"Never mind. Tell you later." Sandy wound the rest of the roll through and removed it from the camera. "Now the light."

Three minutes later he snapped the light-tight lid on the developing tank, put the light back on, and poured developing fluid into the tank. "O.K." he said. "We've got fourteen minutes to wait." He set a timer he found on the shelf. "Might as well do it outside."

They were a tense fourteen minutes, especially for the residents of Eastend. Thompson and Jones talked polite trivialities about fishing, but Anthony and Bateson both answered them briefly, and Ted was scarcely more talkative.

The moment the timer bell sounded, Sandy was on his feet and heading for the darkroom.

"Just pour the developer down the sink," Anthony called after him. "I'll mix a fresh batch when I need it again." He rubbed his hands impatiently. "Another five minutes in the hypo and we'll know," he told Bateson.

When the timer bell rang again it was Anthony who led the way to the darkroom door, where they all crowded close to watch Sandy remove the tank cover. Every eye followed Sandy's deft movements as he pulled the three feet of wet celluloid out of the tank's grooves.

"But there's nothing on it!" Ted said. "The whole thing's blank!"

CHAPTER IX

THE MARKED CLAWS

THE BIG CLOCK in the hall was announcing two o'clock in mournful tones as Mr. Bateson followed the three boys into the kitchen and shut the door. Ted sank into a chair, as if the failure of Sandy's attempt to obtain a satisfactory picture had robbed him of his last shred of energy.

"We'd better all turn in," Mr. Bateson said heavily.

Ken's dark eyes were turned accusingly on Sandy. "Not just yet," he said. "Not until we hear what Sandy's got to say." And when the others looked at him curiously he went on, "All right—tell us. What happened to those two shots you made of the light bulb in the dark-room? Why didn't they come out? You can't blame your flash synchronizer for *those* two blanks."

"Pictures of a light bulb?" Mr. Bateson echoed blankly.

Sandy leaned casually against the table. "That's right," he admitted. "You see, I suspected there was something wrong with the developer, so I took two test shots of the light bulb." He looked complacent. "And I was right. The developer destroyed them both."

"Then *why*," Ken burst out, "did you risk the one important picture in the same developer?"

"I didn't." Calmly Sandy fished in his pocket and pulled out a film cartridge. "That one's still here—waiting to be developed in a solution I'm sure of."

"Oh." Ken's expression changed. "I might have known—"

But Ted interrupted him. "I don't get it," he said, sitting up straight in his chair. "What made you think it wasn't any good?"

"Our plump friend Thompson," Sandy told him. "I didn't like the way he just happened to hold that bottle of cyanide over the open developer jar. A couple of crystals of that stuff are enough to ruin it, so that when the film is put in the hypo it's bleached by the—"

"Please! No lectures," Ken pleaded. "He'd go on like that all night if we let him," he explained to the Batesons. "Not that I don't appreciate your vast knowledge of photographic chemistry," he added hurriedly to Sandy.

"But then there's still a chance!" Ted was saying. "How soon can you develop the picture? Shall I run back to Anthony's and—?"

"No!" Ken almost shouted. "Sorry," he said an instant later. "But I don't think anybody should know about this."

"But *Anthony* wouldn't repeat—" Mr. Bateson protested.

"He suspects everybody, Dad," Ted interrupted him. "He even thinks lobster-pirating pays so well that the *Dolphin* is probably mixed up in it."

"Well, doesn't what Sandy just told us sound as if my

suspicions had some basis?" Ken asked. "You were suspicious of their seamanship yourself," he added. "You wondered how they knew enough to pull us around the headland at full speed."

"That's right. It was a mighty funny thing, Dad." And Ted recounted their hair-raising ride behind the *Dolphin*.

"Hmm. That is curious—when they ask questions as if they'd never been in these parts before," Mr. Bateson mused.

"And there's one other thing, Mr. Bateson," Ken said. He described Jackson's stealthy visit to the *Dolphin* early that evening—a detail he hadn't had the chance to report before.

"At the time," he concluded, "I thought Jackson must be just taking a look around, trying to reassure himself that the *Dolphin* wasn't Coast Guard property. But maybe I was wrong. Maybe he had a date with Thompson and Jones—expected to walk right in—and dashed off when he thought he was about to be caught at it by one of us. Of course the *Dolphin* was dark at the time, but he may have thought that the curtains were drawn."

"It could have been that way," Sandy agreed. "If Jackson and the *Dolphin* are working together on something, they would probably meet secretly like that."

Mr. Bateson rubbed his stubbled chin as if it were all too confusing for him. "But this picture now," he said hopefully, "that might be something we could get our teeth into. When do you think—?"

Sandy looked at the little black metal cylinder in his palm. "We could take it to some town near by and leave it at a drugstore that does developing—though I'd rather not do that. What I'd like to do is to go into New York and develop it myself at the Global News office."

"If we get back from the lobster run early tomorrow, we might drive in then," Ken suggested.

"We may not even go out tomorrow," Mr. Bateson said, "if the fog's as bad as it is now. But I suppose we'd better get a little sleep while we can—in case we do have to make the runs."

Sandy was almost asleep, some fifteen minutes later, when Ken spoke softly from the other bed. "Could Anthony have messed up that developer?"

"Huh?" Sandy turned over, immediately alert again. "Sure. Why not? He had plenty of time alone in there —while he was closing that box of paper. But you don't really think *he's* in this, do you?"

"I don't know what to think," Ken said slowly, "but it opens up interesting possibilities. Suppose Thompson —who's certainly not the friendly innocent he'd like to be taken for—picked up that bottle of cyanide and waved it around just to warn you?"

"Why don't you go to sleep?" Sandy asked, after a lengthy silence. "We'll be up in a couple of hours."

The *Traveler's* engine was running softly when Ken and Sandy ran down the dock the next morning, and Ted was already loosening the bow line.

Mr. Bateson was aboard his boat, making ready to leave. "Take it easy, Ted," he cautioned. "Fog seems to be thinning out now, but she might settle down again. If it gets too thick, come back in."

"Right." Ted motioned Sandy to let go the stern line and the *Traveler* pulled away and headed for the gasoline pump across the harbor. "If it stays like this we'll do all right." He pointed across the water where the shore line was faintly visible.

The *Sea Robin* was ahead of them at the dock, Jackson on the pier and his partner holding the hose nozzle in the boat's tank. The long-armed lobsterman looked down at them as Ted pulled up.

"Hello, sonny." He grinned derisively. "Have trouble getting in last night?"

Ted pointedly ignored him.

"Not sore, are you?" Jackson laughed. "Or maybe you *like* to take joy rides at night."

The man at the pump shut the motor off angrily. "There's your gas, Jackson." He wrote something in his little sales book, tore the sheet out, and thrust it at his customer.

Jackson took it roughly. "Don't see why *I* have to pay cash for my gas. Nobody else does around here."

"You don't have to *buy* your gas here," the proprietor told him evenly. "You can get it somewhere else."

"O.K.—O.K." As Jackson yanked his hand out of his pocket, a few coins and several wooden lobster plugs flew out and clattered on the pier. Immediately Jackson dropped to his knees to recover them, the rest of the money still in his hand. Like a lumbering bear he crawled around, picking up the small items one by one.

"Come on, Jackson," the attendant said impatiently. "I haven't got all day. If a penny turns up later on, I'll save it for you."

"Aw, shut up!" Jackson got to his feet and handed him some money then, but while his change was being counted out he continued to study the wooden planks.

Finally he jumped down into the *Sea Robin* and started off with a rush that set the *Traveler* to rocking.

When the *Traveler* left the pier, in its turn, Ken joined Ted and Sandy at the wheel. "This is what Jackson was so anxious to find," he said. "It fell over on our deck." He opened his hand to show a small lobster plug.

"That!" Ted looked at him incredulously and grinned. "Those things only cost about a half a cent apiece. No—he must have thought there was a quarter or two he'd missed."

Ken shook his head firmly. "He picked up the plugs first—I watched him. As if they were a lot more important than the change."

"It must have been accidental," Ted insisted. "Even Jackson wouldn't worry about a half-cent plug—would he?"

"That's what I'd like to know." Ken turned the plug around so that the blunt end was uppermost. "Could it be because of this?"

There was a round black dot on the end of the plug.

"Does each lobsterman have his own mark?" Ken asked. "I didn't notice any on yours."

Ted took the bit of wood in his hand and studied it. "No," he said slowly, "of course we don't. Plugs are all alike—just plain unpainted wood." He shrugged. "That must be just a spot of tar or something."

"Maybe," Ken agreed. But he put the plug carefully in his pocket and buttoned the flap down.

A boat half a mile off caught their eye as they headed in for bait. "The *Stingray*," Ted remarked. "Anthony's off to an early start."

Thirty minutes later they too were making for the headland over water that looked like a sheet of glass and felt like a well-paved highway. The fog had neither increased nor decreased—visibility held steady at about half a mile—although stray patches sometimes closed in briefly.

Outside the bay they found the water equally still, and the *Traveler*, throttle wide open, cut a clean furrow that spread out behind them until it vanished in the mist.

"I wish a wind would come up," Ted said. "Might blow this away. Otherwise, it'll probably get worse."

During the first hour they found the line and hauled three pots for a total of five good lobsters. Then, just as they picked up the fourth marker, the mist closed suddenly in, blanketing the water so closely that they could only see a hundred feet in any direction.

It took fifteen minutes to find the fifth cork buoy, and almost half an hour to find the sixth. A hole in the fog unexpectedly disclosed the seventh, but the eighth was again the subject of a long search.

When that pot had been rebaited and dropped overboard Ted didn't immediately move on.

"It's getting worse—if anything," he said, studying the surrounding murk. "Maybe we'd better head for home."

Ken counted the lobsters in the tub of sea water. "Only eighteen—won't even pay for your gas, will they? Let's stick it a little longer."

"Well—" Ted considered. "All right. Let's give it another hour."

But by the time they docked the Traveler, at half past

twelve, they had added only another four lobsters to their haul. Mr. Bateson and Hank had already come in, having hauled only six pots before the fog defeated them.

"Anthony docked a couple of minutes ago too," Mr. Bateson said as he helped remove their catch. "Wonder how he made out."

"I wonder too," Ted agreed, "since Anthony's line is right where we found Jackson last night. He hadn't meddled with any of the few pots we could find."

They all wandered over to Anthony's dock when the boats were cleaned and the lobsters packed. Anthony, dumping cracked ice into a case, looked up when they appeared.

"Did Jackson do any damage to your line before we scared him off last night?" Ted asked.

"I don't know," Anthony admitted, picking up the lid for his first case. "I didn't find my entire string. But I hauled twenty-two lobsters out of the fourteen I did find—and that's not so bad."

"Nice ones, too," Ken remarked, glancing down at the hard-shelled crustaceans waving their plugged and helpless claws at each other.

"Yes, they're all right." Anthony put on the lid. "Run to about fifty-five pounds, I guess—enough to make a shipment worth while."

"Going out again if it clears up?" Ted asked.

"I doubt it." Anthony shook his head. "It'll be too late —and anyway I've been promising myself a holiday lately. I've been letting this Jackson business get me too riled up. I ought to get my mind off it for a while. Thought I might drive into New York. Might even deliver these myself for a change," he added, touching the packed case with his booted toe.

"Fine idea," Mr. Bateson agreed. "Do you good."

The boys walked off leisurely until they had turned the corner, and then Ken began to take rapid strides.

"What's the rush?" Sandy demanded.

"Plenty. We're going to New York too—remember?"

"Swell," Ted said. "If you can get that film developed—"

"We'll do that too." Ken stopped at the Bateson driveway and the others looked at him curiously.

"Too?" Sandy echoed.

"That's right. First we're going to do a little investigating—particularly of a restaurant called the Live Lobster."

"What for?" Ted asked. "If you want lobsters to eat, Mom'll give you plenty right here. In fact she—"

"Not the kind Anthony ships," Ken cut in. He hesitated a long moment. "Some of his have plugs with little black dots on them."

CHAPTER X

ENTER VIC SAMSON

THEY MADE THEIR PLANS around the big kitchen table while Mrs. Bateson served lunch. There were six of them at the table—Hank had joined them at Mr. Bateson's invitation.

Ken told the two men of the marked plug he had found at the gasoline dock, and his subsequent discovery of similar plugs in some of Anthony's lobsters.

"Ted thought the one I found had probably been marked by accident," he explained, "that the dot was just a spot of tar or something. But there were three lobsters plugged with pegs exactly like this one"—he held out his hand—"in that case Anthony had just packed—and I could only see the top layer. So there may have been more. I think those marks must mean something—that they're a device to call attention to certain lobsters.

"They also call attention," he added slowly, "to some connection between Jackson and Anthony."

"Oh, but that's—!" Mr. Bateson stopped and sighed heavily. "All right," he said, "I suppose we can't overlook any possibility." Then he shook his head. "I still don't see why anybody would mark a plug. If he wanted to mark a lobster for some reason, why wouldn't he be more direct about it? Just scratch the shell—or something like that?"

"But a marked plug would have the same effect," Sandy pointed out in Ken's defense. "And it wouldn't be noticeable unless a person knew just what to look for."

"The boy's right," Hank said. "Let's stop quibbling. The point is to find out *why*—isn't it?"

"That's what I think," Ken said. "I'm even more curious about the answers to those questions I was asking you last night, Ted."

"What questions?" Ted's father unconsciously echoed his son's query of the previous evening.

"For one thing," Ted told him, after thinking a moment, "he wondered what Jackson was doing the night he used up all his fuel—and still didn't bother our pots."

"Anybody got any ideas?" Ken's eyes circled the table, but there was no reply.

"You also wanted to know why Thompson and Jones were keeping such a close eye on the lobster fleet."

There was no answer to that question either.

"And about Jackson," Ken himself took it up. "How'd he happen to come here, anyway? Does anyone know? Was he driven out of that north shore town where he used to live?"

"Be hard to do that," Mr. Bateson said thoughtfully. "Just as hard for the lobstermen there as it is for us here."

"We could find out about it, though," Hank said unexpectedly. "We could phone Jake Kravcik. He'd know."

"That's so. He might,'"Mr. Bateson agreed.

"I'll go do that now." Hank left the table abruptly.

"Does Jackson own his place here, Mr. Bateson?" Ken went on. "Ted didn't know about that."

"I don't know either." The lobsterman sounded surprised at his own admission. "The county clerk should be able to give us the information—if it has any bearing on this business."

Ken looked a little vague. "It's just a hunch I've got —but I would like to know."

"All right." Mr. Bateson nodded. "I'll find out. And if Jackson doesn't own it himself, I'll find out who does."

"That would be swell." Ken stood up. "Well, I suppose if we're going to New York we ought to be on our way."

"You're not planning to—to get into any trouble there, are you?" Mr. Bateson asked. "I wouldn't want you to—"

Ken shook his head vehemently. "We're certainly not. We'll ask Global News to get a little dope for us. And— I don't know—we might have dinner at the Live Lobster. Nobody could get into trouble doing that, I should think. After all, the customer's always right." He grinned.

Hank returned from his phone call just then. "Jake says Jackson just up and left—but that nobody exactly tried to stop him. Good riddance was the general attitude, I gathered." His thin mouth creased in a rare smile. "Says he's sorry we got stuck with him—but not to send him back."

When the boys were ready to leave, Ken returned to the kitchen to speak again to Mr. Bateson. "Would you keep an eye on Anthony and find out when he leaves? I noticed from upstairs that his car's still in the driveway. We'd like to get to the restaurant before he turns up, so would you phone a message to Global News about it? We'll ask for it when we get in."

"Why, sure—if you think it's important."

"Thanks." Ken gave him the number. "And we'll call you if we learn anything important," he added.

Fortunately, the fog thinned out as they drove away from the water, and by the time the red convertible had covered thirty miles Sandy was able to speed up considerably. At five thirty he was swinging into Queens Boulevard and half an hour later he turned the car over to an attendant in the subterranean garage beneath the Global News office.

They took an elevator directly to the lofty offices of the international news organization, where they were greeted warmly but hastily by Granger, the New York manager.

"Your old man! If he ever gets one of his stories up here during the normal working day, we'll all drop dead of surprise," Granger told Ken, waving a long cablegram. "This has to come *now*—not at noon, of course. Oh, no —that would make it too easy."

"What's up?" Ken asked, glancing at the Peru date line of the story his father had sent.

"Politics. What's up with you?" Granger studied them suspiciously. "You two in trouble again?"

Ken grinned. "Not yet—though we know you can hardly wait. We just want some information. I suppose we ought to have arrived during the normal working day too," he added apologetically. "Must be an inherited characteristic."

"And I want to borrow the darkroom," Sandy added.

"Oh, you do, do you? That's all you want—just our news service and our photographic equipment? Sometimes I think this whole setup is run for your exclusive benefit." Granger sighed elaborately and then grinned. "All right—go see Wilkens. He'll get your dope for you. And you know where the darkroom is." He started out of the room with the cablegram but halted at the door. "Almost forgot," he said over his shoulder. "Mary took a phone call for you. Ask her about it."

The typed message the telephone operator gave them read *Anthony left Eastend at 4:15.*

"Let's step on it," Ken said briskly. "He'll be at the restaurant in a couple of hours. I'll see Wilkens while you're in the darkroom."

Twenty minutes later Ken was rapping at the darkroom door.

"Come in," Sandy called. "Everything's safe."

Ken shut the door carefully behind him, and when his eyes had adjusted to the dim green light, found Sandy sitting on a high stool gently rocking a film tank back and forth.

"Wilkens says we should have come earlier so he could check with some of the city registry offices," Ken said, "but he's doing the best he can by calling a lot of people he knows who might know something." He sat down on another stool. "What gives here?"

"It's in the hypo." Sandy glanced at the timer. "One minute to go."

When the bell rang he lifted the tank's cover, took the spool out of the liquid, held it in a tray of water for a few seconds, and then pulled the two-inch length of film out of the grooves.

"Here it is!" Sandy held the film up so that the green light showed through it, and reached to flip on the white light in order to scan the wet celluloid more carefully.

"Too small for details," he said slowly, "but you can see the two men and a lobster pot."

"The one on the left—Jackson, isn't it?—has something in his hand. Is it a lobster?" Ken peered closely.

"Don't plaster your nose against it." Sandy jerked the film back to safety and dropped it into a tray of water. "I'll give it a minute to wash and then dry it fast."

"How soon can you make a print?"

"About fifteen minutes."

Sandy dried the negative in front of a blast of hot air and then put it in the enlarger, extending the device to its limit to throw an image that measured almost two by three feet.

"Going to be pretty grainy," he muttered, as he focused to sharpen the shadowy outlines. "Probably obscure the fine details. There—guess that's the best I can do."

He slipped a large sheet of sensitive paper into place and made the exposure. A minute later the image appeared on the paper itself, as the developer began to do its work. Sandy rinsed the print, dropped it into the hypo, and a few seconds later turned on the white light.

For a long moment the boys scanned every inch of the *Sea Robin's* aft deck that showed on the print. Jackson and his partner were clearly recognizable, and so was a large lobster in Jackson's hand. But neither the two men nor the lobster was, they knew, the kind of evidence they had hoped for. If there was a marker buoy on the boat anywhere, it had been out of the camera's range.

Grimly the boys studied the slatted lobster pot at the men's feet.

"A lobster pot is a lobster pot," Ken muttered. "Can't prove anything by that."

"Wouldn't you know!" Sandy dropped the print disgustedly back into the hypo. "They're probably standing in front of the buoy."

Ken bent over for one last look. "What's that?" He pointed at an object near Jackson's feet.

Sandy studied it too. Then he took the print out of the solution, rinsed it off, and laid it on the sloping drainboard directly under a light. From a nail on the wall he took a magnifying glass and inspected the print with its help.

"I don't know," he said finally. "Looks like a piece of stovepipe. It's cylindrical, anyway."

"Stovepipe! That doesn't make sense." Ken took the glass from him. "You're right, though," he said a moment later. "That's what it looks like. And that thing behind it looks like a cover for a stovepipe—one of those round old-fashioned tin ones."

Sandy looked once more and nodded, and this time it was he who muttered, "But it doesn't make sense." Finally, he rinsed the print again and laid it on the drying drum. "This print won't last very long—wasn't washed enough."

"If it lasted fifty years it probably wouldn't be any help to us," Ken said, drying his hands on a towel. "Let's go see if Wilkens has picked up something more useful."

Wilkens, whose head was bald above his long, bored face, dropped his phone into its cradle as they entered the office. He indicated chairs and lighted a cigarette. "Couldn't do much," he told them. "But I was lucky enough to catch Gollomb—fellow who does a restaurant column for one of the big papers. He gave me a little stuff—but mostly rumor, he says."

"O.K." Ken told him. "Rumor might be better than nothing."

Wilkens began to read from his notes in a flat monotone. "Live Lobster used to be owned by a Paul Anthony. Likewise used to be located down on the lower east side near the big fish markets. Always well known for good sea food. Sold about two years ago. Reason given—ill health."

Ken nodded. "Go on. So far your rumors fit with ours."

Wilkens paused long enough to stub the cigarette out in an already full ash tray. "Restaurant bought by a syndicate—a corporation—and moved uptown. To a location right around the corner from here, in fact." He glanced up from his notes with what almost seemed a faint show of interest. "Here's the funny thing—Gollomb thinks it's funny, anyway: this syndicate is headed by Vic Samson."

He waited but neither of the boys reacted to the name.

"Samson is a well-known promoter around these parts," Wilkens explained. "He's been mixed up with dubious night clubs, gambling parlors, an occasional race-track scandal. When he took over a restaurant, the sporting circles—as Gollomb calls them—did a lot of tongue wagging."

"Why?" Ken asked quickly. "Is there supposed to be something funny about the restaurant—something shady, I mean?"

"No—no." Wilkens waved a long hand. "Gollomb's idea was that his old pals were surprised Samson should be reduced to such small potatoes." He shrugged. "*You* don't have to think it's funny—just because Gollomb does."

"Well—" Ken looked puzzled. "Anything more about Anthony?" he asked then.

Wilkens got up and crossed the room to get his jacket. "Nothing farther back than the Live Lobster, except that the syndicate—the Sea Food Restaurant Corporation—lists him as its treasurer." He thrust one arm through a sleeve. "That's all I know now. Maybe I can get more tomorrow if you need it."

"What about the *Dolphin?*" Ken reminded him. "Did you—"

"Yeah. Almost forgot." Wilkens, half in and half out of the jacket, returned to his desk and scrambled among loose notes. "Owned by a Robert Thompson, of the Mohawk Club, New York City."

"Is the *Dolphin* registered out of Port Jefferson?" Ken asked. "And what's Thompson do? Who is he?"

Wilkens raised his eyebrows. "Didn't know you wanted his full dossier too." He shrugged. "I'll see what I can do as soon as I come back. Have to go out for a while now."

The phone rang shrilly and Wilkens scooped it up. He listened briefly and then handed it to Ken. "For you. I'll be in later if you want to drop by," he added over his shoulder as he departed.

Ken was already speaking into the instrument. "Oh—Ted. Hello . . . No—no good. Doesn't show the marker. Jackson's holding a lobster and there's a pot on deck all right—but that's no help . . . Huh? He did? Good . . . Who? WHO?" His startled eyes met Sandy's curious ones. "Yes," he added weakly, "we'll be back." He let the phone clatter down.

"What's up?" Sandy demanded.

"Ted says his father checked the ownership of Jackson's house."

"Well—so what? Who owns it?"

"A man named Vic Samson."

CHAPTER XI

HAND-PICKED LOBSTERS

"Vic Samson owns Jackson's house?" Sandy said blankly, as if he doubted the evidence of his ears.

Ken nodded. "*And* the Live Lobster."

They stared at each other. Suddenly the after-hours' quiet of the office was broken by a muted click. Both boys turned instinctively to look at the big clock on the wall, and as they watched, its minute hand clicked forward again.

"Haven't much time," Sandy said then, giving himself a shake. "Anthony should be at the restaurant soon—if that's where he's going."

Ken nodded again, but he wasn't looking at Sandy now. He was staring off into space. "In one way," he said slowly, "this last piece of information clears things up a little. In another way it only adds to the confusion."

"It sure ties Anthony up with Jackson," Sandy admitted.

"And it makes lobster-pirating seem comparatively unimportant," Ken said, beginning to doodle absent-mindedly on Wilkens' telephone pad. "Unless," he added, "there's a lot more money in stolen lobsters than we think."

"What we think isn't important," Sandy pointed out. "But what Mr. Bateson thinks is. And he says lobster-pirating can't be worth much money—even if the restaurant buys them all at good prices."

"I know. And learning about Samson doesn't explain those marked plugs or the fifty-thousand-dollar *Dolphin* that goes off on phony fishing trips in the middle of foggy nights." Ken added an elaborate curlicue to his last doodle.

Sandy stood up. "I say we go take a look at the Live Lobster. We can continue this interesting—if highly useless—conversation on the way."

"O.K. I just want to check something first." Ken put down his pencil and picked up the phone. "Morgue," he said, and waited for the connection. "Have you got a file on Vic Samson?" he asked, when the morgue attendant answered. "Got a picture of him? . . . Good. Will you send it up to Wilkens' office? Thanks."

"Good idea," Sandy approved. "Then we'll at least recognize the gentleman if we meet him."

A few minutes later a copy boy dropped a picture on the desk.

"I only want to look at it," Ken explained. He and Sandy both studied the head-and-shoulders shot of a man in a dinner jacket, turning the print over to check the name on the back. "O.K. Thanks," Ken said finally, handing the picture back.

Then they followed the boy out of the office and took the elevator down to the street.

Ken paused a moment to get his bearings before he turned west. "Should be right in this block."

A minute later they were standing in front of the Live Lobster, looking through the huge plate-glass window at the tastefully arranged display of striped bass, pale curled shrimp, and a great tray of blue-green lobsters. An occasional waving claw assured the public that they were still alive and fresh, and a sign above the tray read *You pick it—We'll broil it.*

Even as they looked a waiter appeared beyond the window, accompanied by two well-dressed diners who thoughtfully chose their lobsters and watched the waiter remove them deftly to a smaller tray for transportation to the kitchen.

"Smart idea," Sandy mused. "That big one there—"

Ken pulled him away from the window and Sandy hastily transferred his thoughts from food.

"I didn't see any with marked plugs," he pointed out.

"You didn't really expect to—in the window, did you?" Ken led the way some twenty feet past the restaurant and urged Sandy into a darkened doorway. "We'll wait here."

Sandy settled himself against the wall. "What are we going to do when Anthony arrives?"

"It'll depend on what he does," Ken replied.

"Then maybe we'd better explore the territory a little first."

Sandy waited for Ken's nod of agreement and they left the doorway together to cross the street, where they could obtain an unobstructed view of the sea food place.

The crosstown street, always crowded with people

during the day, was comparatively deserted now. Only a few pedestrians strolled the sidewalks, although at the end of the block the Fifth Avenue traffic was still heavy. At the opposite end of the block were the brighter lights of glowing Times Square, echoed by the brilliant marquees of the theaters beyond. A mounted policeman passed on his way to the theater section, his horse cantering easily in the center of the street.

The building housing the Live Lobster was only eight stories high and less than fifty feet wide. Flanking it on the east and west were newer and taller structures. The restaurant itself occupied most of the ground floor, but there was enough room left for a doorway leading into a narrow lobby giving entrance to the offices on the upper floors. Two of those floors still showed lighted windows.

"No alley for deliveries," Sandy pointed out. "Do you suppose they carry stuff right in the front door?"

Ken shook his head. "I shouldn't think so. Maybe there's a door in that lobby that leads to the kitchen. Or maybe they use the cellar entrance." He pointed to the pair of iron doors set into the sidewalk and flush with it, just below the restaurant window.

"Sure. That's probably it."

A taxi pulled up in front of the Live Lobster and the couple inside got out and went in. Another group strolling from the direction of Fifth Avenue followed a few minutes later.

"Must be an expensive place to eat," Sandy commented. "All those customers look as if they're used to spending money."

"It's popular too," Ken added. "There's a line waiting

for tables inside." He looked at his watch. "Ten past eight. Wonder if we've already missed Anthony?"

"You stay here," Sandy suggested, "while I take a quick look around inside that lobby."

He had no sooner disappeared through the doorway beside the restaurant window than a station wagon pulled up directly before the Live Lobster. Ken stepped hastily back into a doorway and pretended an absorbed interest in a display of office supplies. But he could see, reflected in the glass, the figure of Anthony emerging from the front seat and walking briskly into the restaurant.

Ken looked around in time to catch Sandy stepping forth from the lobby doorway, to wave his attention to the station wagon, and signal him to remain where he was. The redhead nodded and disappeared again.

Anthony returned to the car and walked around to its rear, where he opened the door and removed two crates which he deposited on the sidewalk. An instant later a bell began to ring, and then, slowly, the iron doors in the sidewalk began to open as the elevator beneath pushed them upward. A young man in white trousers and wrapped in a long white apron stepped off the elevator, helped Anthony put the crates on the small platform, and then returned to it himself, to sink with the crates below the surface of the pavement. The doors closed after him, and Anthony got back in his car and drove off.

Sandy crossed the street in a loping run. "He's just parking the car—heard him say so. He's coming back." He grabbed Ken's arm. "Come on."

Together they hurried to the lobby Sandy had just

left. It was lighted by a single bulb, and one of its two elevators had apparently been left unattended since the bulk of the office occupants had left for the day. Its grilled gates were shut and its light out, but it stood at the street level.

A humming in the other shaft suggested that the second elevator was still in use. The boys glanced up at the indicator above it and watched the arrow mark its descent from the seventh to the sixth floor. It continued downward, and Sandy had only time to point out to Ken the roster of office tenants—it included the listing SEA FOOD RESTAURANT CORPORATION . . . 2nd Floor—before he drew him along to the rear of the lobby.

There was a door there, dimly outlined against the dark wall. Sandy opened it, thrust Ken inside, and pulled it shut. The click of its closing coincided with the rattle of the elevator gate, opening into the lobby.

"Just in time," Sandy muttered.

Ken looked around at the small landing on which they stood, with one flight of stairs leading upward and one down. "What are we supposed to do in here?"

Sandy grinned. "I don't know," he admitted. "I just saw these stairs and thought maybe they'd lead somewhere interesting—one way or the other."

"Let's go down," Ken suggested, after a moment. "The direction the lobsters took."

The stairs descended between narrow concrete walls, turning back on themselves in the middle of the flight. At the midway landing the boys paused, but all they could see ahead of them at the bottom was a closed door like the one they had just come through. They approached it warily, Ken put a careful hand on the knob and turned it. The door opened. Immediately a muted clatter of crockery and the smell of fish and hot oil assailed their senses. Ken peered through a narrow slit for a moment, then pushed the door farther open and slipped through. Sandy followed, pressing the door quietly shut behind himself.

They were in a long cement-floored corridor directly below the lobby. The noise and the smells were coming from an open doorway, some twenty feet from where they stood, in the right wall. Against that wall, between them and the doorway and blocking more than half of the corridor's fifteen-foot width, stood a large pile of crates and cartons, apparently containing supplies for the restaurant.

Shielded by the piled foodstuffs they moved quietly forward down the shadowy passage illuminated only by the light from the open doorway. When they reached the pile itself they edged halfway around it to peer through the door.

The huge kitchen—as large as the restaurant above it—was both noisy and busy. Three men presided at a fifteen-foot stove, bending their high white chefs' caps over first one pot and then another, stooping now and then to clang open the door of the oven or the broiler. A cloud of smoke and steam rose from the stove's vast surface, to be sucked up by exhaust fans into the great hood above it.

A fourth man sat on a low stool, peeling and slicing potatoes from a sack beside him. A fifth washed lettuce in a great sink. And at another, even larger sink, two dishwashers worked elbow-deep in soapy water.

Ken nudged Sandy and directed his eyes to Anthony's two crates of lobsters, standing under a long stainless-steel worktable. So far as the boys could tell the cases had not yet been opened.

One of the chefs opened the broiler door and, with a magnificent gesture, removed three lobsters to great oval plates. Swiftly he added small bowls of melted butter to each platter, set them all on a tray, together with servings of French fried potatoes and green salad, and then deposited the heavily laden tray on a dumb-waiter set into the far wall. As he pulled steadily on the dumb-waiter ropes the tray moved upward out of sight.

Sandy sighed as it disappeared. But when Ken nudged him again he looked obediently toward the rear of the kitchen, as Ken indicated. There a flight of stairs led upward. A pair of black-shoed feet was already in sight, slowly descending. Above them was a pair of well-creased black trousers, and a dinner jacket.

When the man's head came into view Ken caught his breath. It was Vic Samson. The smooth black hair, the handsome dark-eyed countenance was unmistakably the one they had studied in the photograph from the Global News files.

All the chefs nodded their heads deferentially as he appeared.

"Monsieur Vic!" one of them said, breaking into a grin. "*Comment ça va?*"

"None of that French, Charles," Samson returned, grinning in reply. "You know I don't understand it."

The chef shrugged sadly. "I could teach you."

"I've got better things to do." Samson glanced over

the kitchen until his eyes found the lobster crates. "Oh, there they are."

"*Oui.* Er—yes. Monsieur Anthony has brought them in just now," Charles informed him.

"Good." Samson jerked them out from under the table. "Just in time. I'm having a little dinner party and I wanted some good fresh lobsters for it."

"*Bien*—no, no, I mean good. I shall myself pick out the best. How many?"

"Four." Samson pried off the covers. "But I'll pick them myself." He winked at the chef. "Must be extra-special."

"Ha! And you do not think that I—Charles—can pick the good lobster?" He drew himself up. "Perhaps you would wish also to broil them, monsieur?"

Samson grinned again. "No—that's your department. But they're not going to be broiled, Charles. I want them boiled—with your very special sauce, of course."

"But Monsieur Vic! Only when the lobster is broiled —cut so beautifully in two and spread beneath the hot flame—! Ah!" He sighed gustily. "Why—each time that you have the party—you wish them to be only thrown whole into boiling water and—?"

Samson was busy spreading the lobsters out on the table. "Sorry, Charles. I know it breaks your heart. But my guests like only boiled lobsters. What can I do? It's your magnificent sauce, I think," he added.

"Ah, well—it is of course magnificent." And Charles, smiling now, began to poke among the lobsters too.

Quickly Samson set aside one huge one, then a second and third and finally, after careful searching, a fourth. The rest he dumped back into the cases. "These are the ones I want," he said.

Charles, sorrowfully again, shook his head. "They are too large, monsieur. Believe me, the smaller ones have more of the tenderness. No?"

"No," Samson said, patting his shoulder. "My guests like large ones—these."

"Well—I only prepare. I do not eat." Charles shrugged, then looked at the clock on the wall. "In half an hour, monsieur? In the restaurant?"

"No," Samson replied. "Upstairs." And then he left quickly, the way he had come.

Charles threw out his hands dramatically to his fellow chefs. "He is crazy, I think. He chooses the too big lobsters. He wishes that they be boiled. And he does not serve his guests in the so-beautiful restaurant, but in . . ." As he spoke he held up one of the huge lobsters for the other chefs to see.

The waving claws were directly beneath a strong light.

And suddenly Ken and Sandy were backing up the way they had come, Ken's hand tight on Sandy's arm.

"Did you see?" he whispered breathlessly, when they were once more at the far end of the corridor.

Sandy nodded. "A marked plug."

CHAPTER XII

THE FACE IN THE WINDOW

"LET'S GET OUT of here." Ken crept along the piled cases toward the rear of the corridor and the stairway. When they had turned the corner they stopped. "We've got to see what they do with those lobsters," he said.

"The chef said the party wasn't in the restaurant— that it was upstairs. That could mean the office of the Sea Food Restaurant Corporation."

"Probably does. And that's on the second floor, isn't it?"

"That's what the directory said. These stairs go all the way to the top of the building, don't you think?"

Ken nodded. "All we have to do is hope nobody uses them, and that the door on the second floor is open."

Sandy grinned briefly. "And that nobody sees us go through it. Come on."

In spite of all their care their footsteps echoed hollowly in the narrow stair well, but they moved boldly upward. As they rounded the landing on the street floor the whine of machinery startled them momentarily, but an instant later they had both recognized it as the sound of the elevator coming to a stop just beyond the wall enclosing the stairs. The elevator door clanged open and then, after a moment, shut again, and they could hear the cage begin to rise.

They waited briefly and then started upward again, taking the second half of the flight with special caution. At the second-floor landing they paused beside a heavy metal door.

Ken tried the knob and it turned under his hand. Carefully he edged the door open a fraction of an inch and put his eye to the crack.

Immediately they could hear footsteps on the cement floor beyond, but Ken held his pose for a moment before he let the door ease quietly shut.

"Anthony," Ken said to Sandy, framing the single word silently with his lips.

They stood without moving for several long minutes, and then Ken tried the door once more. This time there was silence beyond it, and Ken finally widened the crack. Cautiously he put his head around the door, nodded briefly, and then shoved through with Sandy close behind him.

They were at the rear of the second-floor corridor. The wall on their left was solid, that on their right pierced by four closed doors, the nearest only some ten feet beyond them. Light shone through the frosted glass of its upper half, illuminating the neatly lettered words: SEA FOOD RESTAURANT CORPORATION. From a slightly opened transom above the door drifted an unintelligible murmur of voices.

Motioning to Sandy to wait, Ken moved quickly and silently down the hall, pausing to listen briefly at each of the other three closed and darkened doorways. When he returned to where Sandy stood, just beyond the restaurant corporation's entrance, he clasped his hands together to make a foothold and jerked his head toward the transom.

Sandy understood immediately. He braced his feet solidly and clasped his own hands.

Ken set his foot in the cradle, steadied himself with a firm grip on Sandy's shoulder, and slowly lifted himself. He kept his other hand on the wall to prevent himself from brushing against it.

The transom opened outward, and there was only the narrow slit at the end through which Ken could see. When his eye was finally level with it he peered through for a moment, twisting his head from one side to the other to broaden his field of vision, and then signaled to Sandy to let him down.

On the floor once more he led the way back to the stair well, where they could communicate in comparative safety.

"Well?" Sandy whispered, a little breathless still from the strain of supporting Ken's weight.

"Anthony, Samson, and two other men we've never seen before," Ken reported briefly.

"Doing what?"

"Talking." Ken shrugged. "But at the far end of the room, so I couldn't hear a word." He looked at his watch. "The lobsters will probably be up here pretty soon. I'd like to see what happens then."

Sandy nodded his agreement. "But we can't stand around in the hall—or use the transom—if there's going to be a waiter coming through."

Ken gestured toward the back wall of the stair well and the window it contained. "If there's a fire escape outside that window, with a platform running across the whole building . . ."

Sandy grabbed his arm. "Swell idea! Let's try it."

A moment later they were standing before the window and trying to peer through it. The window itself was grimy, but they could just make out the iron railing a few feet beyond it. So far as they could tell it stretched on in the direction of the corporation's rear-wall windows.

Ken flipped back the catch on the window and then took hold of the handles on the lower sash and heaved. The window didn't budge.

Sandy tried it next, and then they tried together, each clasping one of the metal handholds. But the window remained firmly in place.

"There's still a chance," Ken whispered. "If there's a window like that on every floor, we may find one of them that works. We can come back down on the fire escape."

Together they bounded quietly up to the third-floor landing—but its window too was stuck fast.

On the fourth floor—as grimly quiet as the third—their luck finally changed. The window there slid upward at the first thrust, and Ken reached out to explore the fire escape with his eyes and his hands.

"Seems solid enough," he murmured. "Let's go."

Sandy followed him through.

They left the window open behind them and Ken started down the vibrating iron structure with Sandy close at his heels. On the third-floor platform they stopped to lean out over the railing and study the terrain below. They could see that the fire escape ended in a small courtyard separating the restaurant building from the one backing on the next street. The opposing building was dark, and so was the courtyard. Ken glanced upward briefly; the spidery walk apparently led all the way to the roof.

He took a deep breath and moved slowly down the next flight, arriving on the second-floor platform some ten feet from the rectangle of light he knew must be a window giving on the room he had peered into some minutes before. Then, cautiously, with Sandy behind him, he moved toward it.

Each footfall seemed to grate noisily in the silence. Protected from traffic sounds by the building itself, only the faint clatter of dishes from the kitchen below broke the stillness of the dark.

They were within a few feet of the window when a patch of brilliance suddenly bloomed on the courtyard below, and the rattle of crockery as suddenly increased.

The boys froze into stillness, flat against the wall, as a white-clad figure appeared almost directly below them in the yard. Through the open door behind him warm food-scented air drifted upward.

There was the faint rasp of a match, a flare of fire, and the white-clad figure began leisurely to puff on his cigarette.

Ken allowed himself to breathe again as he realized that it was only one of the kitchen staff enjoying a brief rest away from the heat of his workroom. But neither he nor Sandy dared do more than breathe so long as the figure remained there, its white-capped head less than twenty feet below.

Finally the cigarette was flipped against the far wall of the courtyard in a shower of sparks, the figure turned, and a moment later the kitchen door slammed shut. The space beneath them was once more dark and almost silent.

The boys eased their cramped muscles, and then edged sideways until Ken, in the lead, could peer around the window frame.

He was careful not to draw too close to the glass itself, although he had seen at first glance that it was thick with grime, and he knew that—lighted from within—it probably would effectively screen their dark figures from those inside. The grime on the window was, in fact, so heavy that even the figures in the brilliantly lighted room beyond had a hazy appearance.

The four men he had seen before were still present. Only Samson was in evening clothes. Anthony and the other two wore ordinary dark business suits.

Ken made way for Sandy so that they could both see.

It was like watching a pantomime through a gauze curtain. Anthony, seated at a table facing Samson, was talking earnestly to the restaurant owner, emphasizing the stress of certain phrases with a gesture of his cigarette. Samson, his lips clamped around a cigar, nodded occasionally as if in agreement. The other two men, standing slightly apart, seemed also to be listening to Anthony's words.

But, from where the boys stood, the scene was played

out in silence. The sound of Anthony's voice failed to penetrate the heavy window glass.

Samson suddenly raised his hand and turned toward the other two men. One of them nodded obediently and hastily left the room, to return in a few moments with a folded newspaper. Anthony took it from him, flattened it out on the table and—while Samson watched—drew a pencil from his pocket and circled a spot midway down the page. Again Samson signified agreement by nodding.

Suddenly all four heads raised and turned toward the door. Samson gestured a command and one of the strangers sprang forward to open it.

A waiter appeared and, with brisk efficiency, went to the far wall of the room where he opened a small door. From the dumb-waiter behind it he removed linen and silverware with which he set the table. Four oval platters, each topped by a gleaming chromium cover, were then taken from the dumb-waiter and placed at the four settings.

He opened one of the covers for Samson's inspection. The huge lobster beneath it made a spot of vivid scarlet in the drab businesslike room. Samson nodded, the cover was lowered again, and shortly afterward the rest of the articles on the dumb-waiter—cups and saucers and a large pot of coffee—had been transferred to the table and the waiter departed through the hall door.

Samson moved to that doorway himself when the waiter had gone, turned the key in the lock, and put the key in his pocket. Then he lifted his hand to the bar controlling the transom, and the slanting panel swung shut.

The two strangers—obviously subordinates—had been moving chairs close to the table, and now all four men converged around it.

Anthony picked up one of the shining covers, poked at the lobster beneath it, and grinned at Samson.

Then, handling the hot claw gingerly, Anthony pulled out the plug, dropped it on the plate, and repeated the action with the second claw. Samson gestured impatiently, as if urging him to hurry, and Anthony picked up from beside his plate a nutcracker-like instrument which he clamped around the heavy shell of the first claw.

Sandy's hand tightened on Ken's arm. Both boys were aware of the tense quality in the scene they were watching.

But as they instinctively leaned forward, trying to make out the details of the drama, Samson and the other two men shifted their positions. The two strangers sat down on either side of Anthony, and Samson took the chair opposite him. His broad back entirely concealed the lobster over which Anthony was still apparently working.

Ken drew in his breath with a sharp sense of disappointment. The ritual of dismembering the lobster was apparently of vital importance to the four silent figures beyond the window. Therefore, it was vitally important that he and Sandy should learn its secret.

Ken leaned forward still further.

Suddenly one of the two strangers jumped up from his chair and approached the window.

Ken's muscles jerked.

"Don't move!" Sandy breathed swiftly against his ear.

He was right, Ken knew. Controlling himself with a desperate effort, he held his body rigid. Through the grime and the darkness they might possibly remain invisible—unless they gave themselves away by moving.

The man didn't even glance toward the lower pane, beyond which they crouched. He raised his eyes and his hand toward a dangling cord, jerked it downward, and pulled a heavy window shade down with it. Its creamy opaqueness was as much protection as a brick wall might have been.

But while the boys were still staring at it, in unbelieving relief over their narrow escape, the shade sprang up again, its cord jerking wildly in its wake.

The man, already half turned back toward the table, swung around with the speed of lightning. As if the defective shade were an enemy, he lunged forward to grasp again the still-swinging cord. His face betrayed irritation as it eluded his grasp, and he leaned still closer to the glass to catch it on its next arc.

And then his eyes were staring directly into Ken's. Their two faces, on either side of the glass, were only inches apart.

The man blinked and shook his head, as if trying to persuade himself that it was his own reflection staring back at him. Then suddenly he drew back and his mouth began to open.

The boys never saw the action completed. They were already clattering up the fire escape, past the third-floor window and up another flight. They dove over the open window sill at the fourth-floor landing just as the window below them screeched open.

CHAPTER XIII

BACKS TO THE WALL

SWIFTLY KEN AND SANDY shut the window behind them.

"Up or down?" Sandy breathed.

But Ken didn't need to answer. From below sounded the crash of the stairway door being thrown violently open, and the pound of running footsteps.

"He never opened that window!" The harsh, grating voice was one they had never heard before.

Anthony's voice reached them next. "You stay here. I'll run down and see if he went through the lobby."

Again footsteps pounded, and other voices joined the babble. The hoarse voice cut through to explain: "Anthony's gone down to check the lobby."

Anthony's return was as rapid as his departure. "He didn't go out through the lobby. John's been sitting right there."

"Good."

Anthony went on authoritatively. "I told John not to answer any elevator calls until we tell him to."

"O.K. That means he's in the building and can't get out," Samson said decisively. "Take a floor—each of you—and try every office door."

"Never mind this one," Anthony put in. "Harris, you take the third. Burns'll take the fourth. I'll take the fifth."

"Right," Samson agreed. "I'll stay here."

"O.K., Vic. Make sure nobody gets past you."

"He won't."

Already footsteps were climbing toward them. In the narrow stair well there was no chance for the boys to escape discovery.

Ken jerked his head upward, his lips forming the word "Roof."

Sandy shook his head violently. He eased open the door to the fourth-floor corridor and let it close noiselessly behind them. "We'd be trapped up there," he whispered. "Here we'll have a chance to surprise him when he comes through the door."

But before he had finished speaking, Ken was dragging him along the corridor toward a window in the left wall—the wall that had been blank on the second floor. Ken slid the window open and looked out.

Before him was a narrow space between the restaurant building and the adjoining one—a space caused by a setback in the other building above its second story. The distance between the two brick walls was less than three feet.

There was no time for words. Ken leaped up on the window sill, slid under the raised sash, and stood up on the outer ledge. Then he braced his back against the rough brick of the wall, thrust one foot and then the other against the opposite building, and began to move sideways by alternately hunching his shoulders and edging his feet along.

Before he was more than two feet beyond the window, Sandy too was out on the ledge and the window was closed behind him. A moment later Sandy, employing Ken's tactics, was following him toward the rear of the building.

"Stop!" Sandy's order was the faintest whisper.

Ken had traveled only six feet from the window, and Sandy less than half that distance, but now they both halted. A grotesque shadow had appeared on the opposite wall, framed in the rectangle of light thrown by the window through which they had just come. The shadow wavered, then grew smaller and more distinct —one of the searchers was approaching the window. For an instant the dark outline became the side view of a figure, and Ken swallowed a gasp. There was a gun in that shadowy hand and—in the image projected on the rough brick wall—the gun seemed to point directly at them.

The shadow blurred, and with a grating noise the window slid open. A hand appeared on the sill.

Sandy lifted his own right arm. His intention was clear: if a head appeared through the window that arm would drop like a sledge hammer.

Time seemed suspended in nothingness, like the figures of the boys themselves. Above and below them was dark space. To the rear of the building too were darkness and quiet. And a car appearing briefly in the narrow segment of street, distantly visible far below and to their right, seemed as unreal as a toy.

Then another hand appeared on the sill, and this one held the snub-nosed automatic. But the head remained merely a shadow—and suddenly both hands were withdrawn as a voice called out:

"Anything here, Burns?"

"No. I was just checking this window."

"Don't waste time—there's no fire escape there. Anthony's watching the back stairway now and Samson's taking the car up to check the eighth. We're supposed to check the sixth and seventh. He must be in the building some place—there's no way out. If we don't find him this round we'll get some more of the boys in and go over the whole place with John's passkey—look in every office. If we—"

The slam of the window cut off the rest of the sentence.

"My back," Sandy groaned softly a minute later, when they had both drawn a cautious breath, "will bear the imprint of these bricks as long as I live."

"Crawl back in," Ken said softly. "They've finished this floor for now. But open the window gently."

When they stood in the hallway once more, still breathless and aching from their rigid posture, Sandy muttered, "But with Anthony watching the stairs and the elevator—"

"Look at the indicator!" Ken interrupted quietly, turning Sandy around to show him the metal semicircle above one elevator door. The slowly moving arrow swinging around its curve passed the numeral 2 as they looked, and continued on toward 3.

"Remember they think there's only one of us," Ken said as they moved together toward the heavy door beneath that swinging arrow. Ken pressed the elevator button as Sandy took up a position on the opposite side of the door. "Flatten out," Ken added, and they both pressed their bodies back against the wall.

The car overshot the mark under Samson's inexpert handling, halted midway between the fourth and fifth floors, started down again, overshot once more, and was finally stopped even with the fourth floor.

"Burns?" Samson asked quietly through the still-closed door.

Ken rapped on the panel and spoke in a hoarse whisper. "Got him cornered."

The inner gate rattled open instantly and the solid outer panel slid back.

"Burns? Where—?"

"Shh!"

Samson's head came forward through the opening, turned in the direction of Ken's whisper, and suddenly jerked back. But he hadn't reacted fast enough.

Ken's uppercut reached the well-shaven chin just as Sandy's pile-driver blow struck the top of the sleek head. Samson's slightly opened mouth closed with a loud click and his body slumped to the floor across the open doorway.

Hastily the boys dragged him back inside the car and Ken propped him up in a corner while Sandy shut the door and the gate.

"Take her up," Ken said. "That's where they're expecting her now."

Sandy studied the lever briefly, decided which way it ought to be moved, and jammed it home. The car started with a lurch.

There was pounding at the sixth floor. Burns's hoarse

voice reached them even before the roof of the car passed the floor level. "Hey! Did you call me?"

"Keep her going," Ken said. "Right to the eight."

"Hey! Samson!" The pounding on the door became more insistent as they rose above it.

A buzzer sounded in the car and the indicator in front of Sandy flashed white for the seventh floor. Then the buzzer went off again and the sixth-floor light flashed.

Sandy ignored the signals and tried to stop the car level with the eighth floor, but he was three feet above it when the car jerked to a halt. "Watch your step," he said, starting to move the lever to DOWN.

"Hold it!" Ken pulled the gate open. Directly in front of him, at eye level, was the mechanism that turned the eighth-floor indicator. "See this rope? It turns all the indicators as the car moves." The penknife in his hand flashed once and then once more. The rope parted. "Take it down—fast. As far as the indicators are concerned, we'll still be at the top."

Sandy slid the gate shut and moved the control lever. The car descended smoothly.

"Take it right down to the cellar," Ken said as they passed the sixth floor where Burns still shouted at the door. There was silence at the fifth floor, at the fourth, and at the third, but they could hear Anthony's roaring voice when they passed the main floor.

"John—don't let anyone out here! I'm going down to the cellar!"

A second later the car reached the basement, and even before it stopped bouncing up and down on the bumper springs, Sandy had opened the gate and leaped out. Ken paused only long enough to shift the control lever to UP. When he closed the gate behind him, the car started its return journey with no hand at the helm.

There was time only to dive behind a row of ash cans before Anthony's pounding feet came down the basement corridor. He raced past the pile of restaurant supplies and skidded to a stop at the foot of the elevator shaft. The whining of the machinery indicated that the car was ascending again. Anthony stood a moment irresolute, then he turned and ran back the way he had come.

"The lobby is guarded," Sandy reminded Ken as they straightened up.

"Fine." Ken led the way toward the front of the building, skirting more ash cans, packing cases, and piles of old newspapers. "It ought to be here some place."

"What?"

"Here it is." Ken pointed to the small freight elevator that ran up to the sidewalk. "Get on."

Sandy complied dubiously. "How do you know who's out there waiting for us?"

Ken pressed the control button and the small platform jerked into motion. "Can't be any worse than what's waiting for us back there."

Overhead the warning bell began to ring as the upper framework of the car approached the iron doors in the sidewalk. The car was in no hurry—it inched its way upward, the clamor of the bell so loud in the boys' ears that it seemed certain all four men would be summoned by its sound.

The doors were open wide now, although the car still

had two feet to rise, and the glare from the windows of the restaurant enveloped them in light and heat.

They tensed their leg muscles prepared to make a dash for it, but there was no one to greet them—no one but a lone pedestrian who looked at them curiously for a moment before continuing on his way.

The boys stepped off the platform casually, fighting down an impulse to run as fast as they could. They crossed the street and sauntered toward Fifth Avenue, stealing anxious glances over their shoulders.

"Relax," Ken said. "They're looking for one man—not two."

A hundred feet farther on they passed a drugstore ablaze with lights and crowded with people. Sandy grabbed Ken's arm and thrust him through the revolving door.

"We don't have to hide," Ken protested when Sandy joined him.

"Maybe not." Sandy pointed to a cluster of tables and booths. "But I'm hungry."

CHAPTER XIV

THOMPSON TURNS TRAILER

THEY SLID into a corner booth in the drugstore, as far as possible from the front door. The padded seat back was protectingly high, and comfortably soft in contrast to the rough bricks they had pressed against a few minutes before.

Sandy picked up a menu even as he settled himself. "Not much of an assortment," he said, studying it in the light of the small table lamp. "Guess we'll have to take hamburgers—with French fries, of course. And pie and stuff."

Ken was shaking his head.

"No?" Sandy asked. "You'd rather have a Western sandwich or—?"

"I mean I can't figure you out," Ken explained. "A few minutes ago we were on the wrong end of a pretty determined man hunt. Were you thinking about food then too—while we were wedged in between those buildings, for example?"

Sandy stared at him in amazement. "Of course not! I was giving my whole attention to being scared stiff. But the thing is," he explained, "I'm the simple type. I can only do one thing at a time. When I'm scared I'm not hungry. But when—"

"When you're not scared, you are," Ken finished.

"Sure. Elementary." Sandy grinned. "So what'll it be? Hamburgers?"

"I guess so. Two, and some coffee. We could use some soap and water too," Ken added, glancing down at his hands.

"We sure could. Let's just order first."

Ten minutes later, considerably cleaner, they tackled well-filled plates and steaming cups. As Sandy spread ketchup over his second hamburger he sighed.

"I'm beginning to feel practically human now," he said. "Let's talk."

Ken looked over his coffee cup. "We sure have a wide variety of topics to choose from: marked claws, spoiled film, stolen lobsters, a fancy restaurant, a fifty-thousand-dollar boat, race-track owner turned restaurant proprietor—"

"Also restaurant owner turned lobster fisherman, sport fishermen who like to fish in the fog with only twenty feet of line, amateur navigators who can find a harbor in pea soup at full speed . . ." Sandy ran down. "What's the use? It doesn't add up to anything." He bit disgustedly into his hamburger.

"You're wrong about that," Ken answered. "It must add up to something—or all these people wouldn't be doing it."

"Doing what?"

"Whatever they're doing." Ken sighed. "But you're right, of course, if you mean we don't know what it adds up to."

Sandy didn't answer until his plate was empty. "Now I can give this my full attention," he said then, briskly. "You must still be hungry or you wouldn't be so depressed. Very unlike you to admit you don't know anything."

"I didn't—"

Sandy ignored him. "We do know that Jackson's stealing lobsters. We know that Anthony's marking certain lobsters and sending them to a restaurant which he once owned and in which he still has an interest. We—"

"Sure," Ken interrupted. "We know something about all of them—all the parts of the puzzle. But we can't put them together to make sense. It's easy enough to say that Anthony and Samson are connected, and that Jackson must be involved somehow with them too—or Samson probably wouldn't own his house. But *why?* And what's Thompson after? Lobsters? Pretty unlikely."

Sandy looked at his wrist watch and gulped the last of his coffee. "Get a move on. Here I am, ready to sacrifice dessert in order to get back to Global and see if Wilkens has anything more for us about Thompson, and you—"

Ken hastily picked up his own cup. "You're right. Maybe one more little fact is all we need to clear up the thing. O.K. I'm ready."

In spite of the well-lighted thoroughfare outside the drugstore, and the conviction that if anybody had followed them out of the Live Lobster they would have been aware of it by now, both boys threw nervous glances back over their shoulders as they walked rapidly toward Fifth Avenue. But they reached the Global office without incident.

Wilkens eyed them incuriously. "You can't expect to get decent answers to your questions at this time of night," he said in his usual bored tone. "I've been bothering a lot of people and they didn't enjoy it—and I still don't know much. Got a call in now for our yachting expert. He's checking the Port Jefferson registrations. Boat like the *Dolphin* ought to be pretty well known, at least in her own neighborhood."

He lighted a fresh cigarette. "Checked the police department for car registrations. A man who owns a big boat ought to have at least one car."

"That was a swell idea," Sandy told him. "If you found out where his car is registered—"

"I didn't. It isn't. Far as I can discover he doesn't own a car—at least not one registered in New York, New Jersey, or Connecticut. However," Wilkens went on, not waiting to note their reaction to this piece of news, "according to the phone books of the five boroughs of New York, six Robert Thompsons reside in this vicinity."

"Six!" Sandy groaned.

Wilkens continued without comment. "Four of them live in sections where people don't even have toy boats —let alone yachts. The other two don't own yachts either—or so they told me when I called. And—"

The phone rang and Wilkens broke off to answer, picking it up with his left hand while his right automatically reached for a fat black copy pencil. But he didn't take notes as he listened. And he made no reply to the speaker except a brief "Thanks" before he hung up.

This time, however, when he looked up at the boys there was a faint show of curiosity in his glance. "Sure

you didn't get a bum steer?" he ask. "Dryden—our
yachting man—says none of the clubs at Port Jefferson
ever heard of the *Dolphin*. Also says he doesn't understand why he's never heard of it himself, if it's as im-
pressive a boat as you say it is. Dryden knows his business."

Wilkens' eyes narrowed. "If I hadn't checked the
registration myself," he added, "I'd say there was no
such craft afloat."

"I know he told us his home port was Port Jefferson,"
Ken said thoughtfully. "But he could have been deliberately throwing us off the track."

"I could try the insurance companies—and see what
I can find out from the Mohawk Club." But Wilkens
had already turned to his typewriter.

The boys took the hint.

"O.K. If it wouldn't be too much trouble," Ken said,
starting for the door.

"Phone me—at some decent hour tomorrow." Wilkens' farewell was a machine-gun burst of noise from
his battered machine.

Out in the hall they turned toward the darkroom
where Sandy retrieved the dry print. "We might be
complicating this whole thing ourselves," he said as
they walked toward the elevator. "Take out the *Dolphin*, and the other factors fit together a lot better."

"This is no time to take out the *Dolphin*," Ken
pointed out. "She's more mysterious now than ever."

"But look. There was probably a mysterious robbery
in Timbuktu yesterday—but it doesn't necessarily tie in
with our problem. Forget the *Dolphin* for a minute.
Anthony and Jackson could be in cahoots in some big-

scale lobster-stealing deal. Maybe Samson's outfit has a whole chain of restaurants—big enough so that it makes the lobster-pirating profitable." He punched the button again.

"Sure, maybe he has," Ken agreed. "But that doesn't solve everything. What about the marked claws? If they're just stealing lobsters, why mark certain claws?"

Sandy shrugged just as the elevator door slid open. They got in and leaned wearily against the back wall as the car descended.

"Down to the garage, please," Ken said.

"This car doesn't go below the main floor," the operator told them. "You'll have to take car number three from there."

"O.K. Thanks."

A moment later they were crossing the main lobby to the opposite bank of elevators when a newspaper stand caught Ken's eye.

"Hold it," he said. "That newspaper Anthony and Samson were so interested in, while we were out on the fire escape. Any chance that we can identify it? I'm pretty sure it wasn't a tabloid size," he added thoughtfully, eying the neat piles of newsprint before him.

"Right," Sandy agreed. "And I'm pretty sure the page he was looking at had a big ad for some kind of a cigar —I remember the long torpedo shape up in the corner."

"That's good enough." Ken scooped up a copy of every full-size paper on the stand and dropped some coins in exchange.

In a quiet corner of the lobby he divided the pile with Sandy.

Hurriedly they began to leaf through the unwieldy

sheets, dropping each issue into a waste container as they finished. Sandy looked up as he inspected a page toward the back of his last paper.

"This is it, I think." He held it out for Ken's inspection, indicating the big black representation of a cigar in an upper corner.

Ken's eyes scanned the sheet rapidly, and then focused on a double-column heading near the middle of the page. His forefinger jabbed at it. "Look familiar?"

" 'Shipping and Mails,' " Sandy read. "Sure." His voice had quickened. "Through the window of the *Dolphin* that time—there was a circle around—" And then he stopped. "But it might have been the next column they were all so interested in—the tide tables."

Ken nodded. "Could have been. But if they *were* looking up incoming ships—and Thompson was too—"

"Ahoy, *Dolphin*," Sandy said resignedly. "And just when I was trying to get you to forget her for a while. Come on. Let's get back to Eastend and see what gives there."

The elevator dropped two stories into the underground garage and they stepped out into its gasoline-laden atmosphere. The great subterranean parking area was jammed with the cars of theatergoers, but since the big exodus would not begin until after eleven, the half-dozen attendants were lounging around the small office near the exit.

The boys walked toward the group of men, and Ken held up his wallet so that the Global press card showed clearly.

One of the attendants nodded. "Which one?"

"Red convertible," Ken told him.

The attendant sighed. "Probably buried pretty deep by now." But he moved off immediately, down a lane between two rows of closely packed vehicles, toward the section reserved for Global cars. "After office hours we use this space for regular customers," he explained.

The convertible was wedged so tightly between two other cars that there wasn't more than a few inches of clearance on either side.

"You'd better wait in the aisle. I'll get her out," the attendant said. "No use you getting dirty too."

"Thanks," Sandy said. He touched Ken's arm. "Come on—move out of the way."

But Ken didn't hear him. His eyes were fastened on the spot by the office which they had left a moment before. As Sandy followed his glance a familiar voice said, "It's a station wagon. Here's the check."

"Anthony!" Sandy breathed.

"Duck!" Ken commanded.

And immediately, ignoring the dust the attendant had warned them of, they squeezed between two cars in the same row in which the convertible stood. Ken craned his neck to peer through the rear window of the car on their left.

Two cars beyond where they stood the convertible began to back slowly out. When its front end was clear, the attendant cut the wheels hard. But the amount of space was small for the car's size, and the red car moved forward and back some ten times before it finally was able to swing free into the aisle, facing the exit.

"Want to take it now?" The attendant slid from behind the wheel.

"Sure." Ken let Sandy take the driver's place. "Thanks

a lot," he added. He slipped in beside Sandy. "Stall until the station wagon leaves."

But almost at that moment Anthony's car swung into the aisle far ahead, and Anthony took the wheel. The station wagon coughed up a cloud of blue smoke, its wheels began to turn, and it climbed up the ramp into the street beyond.

Before Anthony's front bumper had crossed the low curbing, the red convertible had reached the office cubicle at the foot of the ramp. As it started up the incline they could see the station wagon swing east into the thoroughfare.

Sandy reached the top and spun the steering wheel to follow. He had just made the turn when Ken grabbed his arm.

"Hold it!"

Sandy stepped hard on the brake pedal and the tires squealed on the paving as the wheels locked. A shabby coupé, which had been parked at the curb on the other side of the exit, had suddenly sprung into life and shot past the great garage doorway.

Neither of the boys could identify the driver. But the second man in the coupé's front seat was clearly illuminated in the glow of the huge overhead garage sign.

"Thompson!" Sandy exclaimed as they stared blankly at the coupé's rear end. "And trailing Anthony!"

Ken grinned faintly. "We were going to count him out. Remember?"

"Now we're counting him in." Sandy released the brake and the red convertible began to move down the street in the coupé's wake. "And all we have to do is figure out what he's doing here."

CHAPTER XV

FORCED OFF THE ROAD

THE RED LIGHT stopped them. Two cars ahead of them the coupé was also brought to a halt, directly behind Anthony's station wagon.

"Thompson's following Anthony," Sandy muttered. "We're following Thompson. Wonder who's following us."

Ken looked back. "Nobody—so far as I can tell," he reported.

"What do we do? Stick with the parade—or head back to Eastend?"

"That's probably where they're going," Ken pointed out.

The light changed and the cavalcade moved. Anthony turned north for one block, waited for the light to change, and then turned again—east this time, back toward Fifth Avenue. Thompson's coupé and the red convertible followed.

"Then he's *not* going back to Eastend," Sandy said, making the last turn. "This isn't the way to the Queens Midtown Tunnel."

"Maybe Anthony uses the Triboro Bridge," Ken suggested. "It's just as good."

Still trailing Anthony, the coupé and the convertible turned north again on Fifth Avenue and continued up that broad thoroughfare as far as Seventy-ninth Street. There Anthony swung eastward and remained on the crosstown street until he reached the East River Drive. When he turned northward on the Drive, Thompson in the coupé was two cars behind him, and the boys were three cars behind the coupé.

"Better close up a little," Ken suggested. "Cars move right along on this highway—we don't want to lose them."

Sandy cast a glance in the rear-view mirror and then began to edge out into the left lane.

Suddenly a horn blast ripped out from behind, and the next instant a heavy sedan hurtled past them. It had cut far out to the left to skirt the convertible, and now it swung sharply to the right to avoid the concrete island dividing the highway into two lanes. Sandy braked swiftly as it crossed his path. The sedan straightened with a lurch that set the low heavy body rocking, and then cut on over into the right lane directly behind the coupé.

"Wow!" Sandy said, letting the convertible pick up speed again. "What a fool! Drivers like that shouldn't be allowed on the road." He glanced at Ken. "I'd just as soon keep him in front of us, if it's all the same to you."

Ken nodded. "I guess we can still watch our friends from here."

Sandy edged slightly out of line, so that he could look

up ahead to Anthony's taillight. "I've got my eye on him," he assured Ken.

Several minutes later Anthony's direction indicator began to blink for a left turn, and almost immediately the station wagon pulled into the left lane and began to slow down. The coupé followed suit.

Sandy put his arm out and veered left. Ahead of him the heavy sedan swung into the left lane too, and a moment later they all stopped at the Ninety-sixth Street traffic light, waiting for a break in the southbound traffic.

When the light changed, the station wagon, the coupé, the sedan, and the convertible headed west on Ninety-sixth Street. In that same order they stopped for a red light at First Avenue, and when the signal changed to green, Anthony continued westward, followed by the coupé. The sedan turned left on First Avenue and headed south.

"That's a relief," Sandy muttered, cautiously closing the gap the sedan had left. "I don't like to drive in the same city with guys like that."

Ken's mind was on something else. "Something fishy here," he said. "He's not heading for the Triboro Bridge, either. What's Anthony doing—just cruising around New York City?"

Sandy saw the red light up ahead at Second Avenue, and began to slow down so that he wouldn't be forced to halt directly behind the coupé. But the light changed a moment later, and Sandy stepped on the accelerator again. Before the convertible had reached the crossing, Anthony had turned north on Second Avenue and the coupé swung after him.

"Now what?" Sandy wondered aloud, pulling at his own wheel.

"No!" Ken said, grabbing at the wheel himself. "Don't turn! Straight ahead!"

Obediently Sandy kept the car in line, cutting directly across Second Avenue. But his voice was indignant.

"What's the idea?" he demanded. "Didn't you see—?"

"That sedan—the one that almost sideswiped us," Ken broke in, "is waiting there at the corner!"

"Waiting?" Sandy repeated incredulously. "But he—"

Ken was looking through the rear window. "He's still there—on Second Avenue, heading the same way Anthony and Thompson went."

"But how'd he get there?" Sandy asked, braking the convertible's crawl to a full stop in Ninety-sixth Street.

"Probably went down to Ninety-fifth, turned right on a red light, and cut up Second Avenue in time to be there ahead of us."

"But why? What's he—?"

"That's what I want to know." Ken was still looking out the rear window. "There's no one behind us right now. Take a chance on a U-turn."

Sandy swung the car around and headed it eastward.

"And now park," Ken told him, gesturing toward the curb some fifty feet from the corner.

"There he is," Sandy said, getting his first sight of the sedan still standing where Ken had sighted it on Second Avenue. "Seems to be waiting for somebody— he could move if he wants to. The light's green."

"I think we're waiting for somebody too." Ken looked back once more. "And here they come."

An instant later Anthony's station wagon swept by, only to halt at the corner for a red light. Behind it the coupé, too, came to a stop.

"There goes the sedan," Sandy said. Together they watched it swing eastward around the corner, into the street they were on.

When the light changed, Anthony moved after it, the coupé still behind him.

"We bring up the rear?" Sandy asked, swinging into the lane of traffic.

"Right."

At the First Avenue crossing they were all held up by the light; the sedan first, then the station wagon, then the coupé, and last the convertible.

In that same order they traversed the next crosstown block, and back at the East River Drive they all turned north.

Sandy eased his foot off the gas, to widen the distance between themselves and Thompson's coupé.

"Well," he said, "looks like it's the Triboro Bridge after all. But what was the idea of that senseless side trip?"

"I think Anthony knows he's being trailed," Ken answered. "He took that detour just to see if the coupé would stick with him—and it did."

"And what about the sedan?"

"I don't know," Ken admitted. "Maybe he's an innocent bystander—but I've got a hunch he's part of the picture too."

Still fourth in the procession, they climbed the complicated approaches to the Triboro Bridge, paid the toll, and a few minutes later were on Long Island's Grand

Central Parkway. On their left were the huge hangars of LaGuardia airport, thousands of red lights defining the wide expanse of runways. Here, on the more open road, Sandy allowed a car to come between the red convertible and the coupé.

A horn sounded up ahead, sounded again, and the stop light on the car just in front of them blinked on and off. Suddenly that car swerved to the left and speeded up to shoot around a slowly moving vehicle. Sandy followed.

It was the sedan, almost crawling now, that they found themselves passing.

"I think maybe you were wrong," Sandy said with satisfaction as the sedan fell farther and farther behind.

"Get a move on," Ken advised. "Thompson's pulling ahead."

Sandy swung around the car in front and pulled back into line directly behind the coupé. "From here on out everybody will be traveling faster," he pointed out.

"I suppose so. We—"

Ken's voice was lost in the loud blast of a horn from the rear. Headlights behind them flashed on and off twice.

The sedan was edging up on them again, its speed increasing steadily. It was already in the left lane and traveling fast.

"Well! What do you—!" Sandy stepped harder on the gas.

"No!" Ken said suddenly. "Let him pass!" His voice was tense, and he leaned forward, bracing his hand against the dashboard.

Sandy's jaw clenched, but he eased his foot up, and

almost immediately the sedan slid past and began to close in on the coupé.

It happened fast. Anthony's station wagon had shot ahead like a rocket, stretching the distance between itself and the coupé from twenty feet to fifty, and then to seventy-five. The sedan let go with its horn again and leaped ahead as if to follow.

"Look out!" Ken shouted.

The sedan had veered sharply to the right—its long hood cutting straight in front of the coupé. The coupé's wheels swiveled right, and an instant later the small car leaped the low curbing onto the wide lawn flanking the parkway. It bounced high as the rear wheels lurched over the barrier, skidded briefly on the grass, and then plunged through a row of low bushes to crash into the rustic fence beyond. There was a loud tinkle of glass as the headlights shattered.

That was all the boys saw. Sandy had pulled the car into the left lane, with a screech of tires. Now he pulled it back just as roughly. But they were rounding a curve and Ken could no longer sight the coupé even through the rear windows.

The sedan had already swung wide around Anthony's station wagon and shot ahead. The station wagon slowed, as Sandy closed in on it, and edged into the exact middle of the highway, as if to block pursuit.

Ken straightened in his seat. "Fall way back," he said. "Don't let him think we're chasing the sedan."

Sandy eased up on the gas and drew the back of his hand across his forehead. He let out his breath on a long, low whistle. "That's rough playing," he said then. "Do you think they got hurt—back there?"

"I shouldn't think so. Bruised maybe. But the car was still right side up."

"Probably not in running order, though," Sandy pointed out.

"Probably not—we heard the headlights go."

"So that puts Mr. Thompson out of the running—at least temporarily—which was apparently the idea." Sandy gestured down the road ahead. "Anthony's taking his time now. Look at him."

The station wagon, back on the right side of the road again, was moving at a slow, sedate pace. There was no longer any sign of the sedan.

Behind them the traffic, momentarily slowed by the near-collision, was closing in again and passing both the convertible and the station wagon. Then a car slid in between them, soon followed by a second.

And although Sandy was careful never to let Anthony get entirely out of sight, the trip continued uneventfully. Anthony took the proper turns for Eastend, and maintained his steady pace until he pulled into a gas station at Smithtown.

Sandy drove slowly past. "He's getting gas all right. Should we wait?"

Ken shook his head. "I think the excitement's over for tonight. He seems to be heading straight for home. We might as well too."

Two hours later they turned into the Bateson driveway. Sandy switched off his lights and let the car coast past the house, entirely darkened except for a light in the front hallway apparently left for their convenience. In the shadows of the shed the convertible came to a halt and the boys got out, closing the doors softly and instinctively keeping their voices down. All of Eastend seemed peacefully asleep.

They had started back toward the house when the noise of an approaching car reached them, faintly at first and then growing stronger. Headlights winked through the trees. The boys watched as the lights swung in an arc and then blinked out.

"Anthony," Ken said quietly. "He—"

He broke off to listen to the sound of another car, and they both watched the second pair of headlights appear. It followed the same curving course the first had taken, and then it too vanished.

"Pretty late for visitors," Sandy muttered. "What—?"

Ken silenced him with a hand on his arm. "Let's see if the *Dolphin* is still around," he breathed, and led the way around the shed and, stepping softly on the grass, down toward the dock.

They were about to set foot on the wooden planking when the sound of other footsteps stopped them—footsteps somewhere ahead in the shadowy darkness of the pier's end.

"Well," a voice said, quietly but clearly, "he's here. Let's get ready to move out."

It was Jones's voice, Ken realized.

"Not *he*," another voice answered. "*They*." There was a faint chuckle behind the word. "We're going to have a lot of company tonight."

Footsteps sounded again. A cabin door opened and closed gently, and then there was silence.

"That was Thompson!" Ken said.

"And how in the world did he get here so fast?" Sandy asked.

CHAPTER XVI

STOWAWAYS

FOR A LONG MOMENT Ken could think of nothing but the question that Sandy had just put into words: How *had* Thompson reached Eastend so quickly?

Then he decided that the appearance of Thompson wasn't important at the moment. The problem that had to be solved quickly was not how Thompson had managed to get here, but what he intended to do now. Jones's quiet "Let's get ready to move out" echoed again in Ken's ears, followed by Thompson's "We're going to have a lot of company tonight."

"Come on," Ken said quietly, touching Sandy's arm. "Let's go see if Anthony is part of the 'company.'"

They stepped into the shadow of the trees dotting the space between Bateson's house and Anthony's, glad of the soft turf that swallowed their footsteps. When they reached the hedge that screened Anthony's house they stopped. No light showed anywhere.

Ken nudged Sandy and began to move again, this time toward the water. Fifty feet farther they came to the edge of the hedge and cut around it, between the house and the shed that loomed darkly less than ten yards away.

Suddenly Ken stopped. Out of the corner of his eye he had caught a faint glimmer of light from the house— as if a drawn curtain had been momentarily stirred, revealing briefly the glow behind it.

The boys stood rigid, waiting, ears alert for the slightest sound, eyes glued to Anthony's back door. A rope creaked somewhere from the direction of Anthony's dock, and the water lapped gently at the piling, but there was no other noise and no visible movement.

Ken looked cautiously around. Their eyes were completely adjusted to the darkness by now, and details were becoming more visible. Anthony's station wagon was a dim silhouette near the shed, and behind it was the outline of another vehicle. Sandy, seeing it too, left Ken for a moment and then silently returned.

"Looks like the same sedan," he whispered.

The sliver of light appeared again at one of Anthony's windows, disappeared immediately, and then there was the soft rattle of a knob.

The boys ducked swiftly back to the hedge and dropped flat on the ground behind it. Anthony's back door creaked open and shut.

"Hold it a minute." Anthony's voice was low-pitched but perfectly audible. "Wait until we can see. I don't want to use any light."

"The whole town's dead asleep." The answer was an irritable growl.

"The skipper of the *Dolphin* might have insomnia— wondering what's happened to his friend."

"Let him wonder. As long as he stays tied up at—"

"But he might not," Anthony broke in authoritatively. "We've got to play it safe—assume he may go out alone if he gets suspicious."

"What is this?" The growl dropped a note, ominously. "I risk my neck to put the fat one out of the picture, and apparently I could have saved myself the trouble."

"Take it easy. Even if the worst happens, one man on that boat would be less trouble to handle than two. Now remember, Burns, we're depending on you. Don't let Jackson pull the same fool stunt he did the other night—letting someone come close enough to take a picture! Why, if I hadn't fixed that developer—"

"O.K. So you're a genius," the growl cut in. "Congratulate yourself later."

When Anthony spoke again his voice was clipped, and there was a new hardness in it. "You're to do all the work *inside* the cabin, and to get rid of everything as fast as you can."

"I know. I know."

"Give me a twenty-five minute headstart, and remember the signal."

"I *know*." There was a short unpleasant laugh. "You don't have to spell it out for me. I know this is the big haul—and probably the last one. But I've handled plenty of tougher assignments than this. I took care of your government man for you, didn't I? And I know the rest of my routine."

"But, Burns, I—"

Burns ignored the interruption. "If the *Dolphin* doesn't take off after you—if we've still got to consider that possibility—I'm to wait ten minutes and then give you three flashlight blinks from the dock. Then Jackson and I take off and head east, with plenty of noise—in case anybody's interested in following."

"Right. But if the *Dolphin* does follow me, I'll draw her off to the east and you'll have to make the pickup."

There was the sound of footsteps and a new voice. Ken recognized it as that of Anthony's assistant on the *Stingray*. "You ready?"

"Yes," Anthony answered. "Got the lobsters on board?"

"Yep. Ten big ones—just like you said."

"Good. O.K., Burns, you'd better get over to Jackson's."

"I'm on my way."

"Let's go."

One pair of footsteps receded rapidly. But Anthony and his assistant walked within a few feet of where the boys lay, before the quiet crunch of gravel indicated that they had passed the corner of the shed. An instant later there was the hollow sound of heels on planking. The two men had reached the dock.

"So Thompson's a government man!" Sandy breathed incredulously. "A couple of fine detectives we are!"

"Come on." Ken was already moving. "We've got to warn him that Anthony's planning a wild-goose chase."

They made their way back to the Bateson driveway as quickly as they could, but even before they reached it they heard the vibrant sound of the *Stingray's* exhaust. They dropped caution then, tearing noisily toward the Bateson dock.

But the *Dolphin* wasn't in sight. There was only a

faint smell of gasoline fumes and the disturbed lapping of water against the pilings to tell of her recent departure.

And the *Stingray* was already out in the harbor. She was moving without lights, but her course could be followed by the sound of her exhaust. She was unmistakably making for the inlet. And probably, Ken thought, the *Dolphin* was taking the same route.

"Would it do any good to yell?" Sandy suggested.

"We'd warn Anthony too," Ken pointed out. He looked at his watch. "Keep an eye on the blinker. I'll be right back."

Less than a minute later he returned to Sandy's side. "Have they gone by yet?"

"Not—" Sandy stopped and pointed. At that very moment the *Stingray* was sliding past the intermittent beam of the inlet marker, a ghostly outline against the faintly starlit water.

Long tense seconds passed, and then the *Dolphin's* low sleek silhouette moved past the same point.

Ken looked once more at his watch. "Four more minutes."

Sandy stared at him blankly. "Four more until what?"

"Until it's time to signal that the *Dolphin* isn't following Anthony." Ken was watching the second hand.

"But it is!"

"Sure. And Burns probably knows it." Ken glanced up briefly. "He's the man who looked out that window with the gun in his hand while we were wedged between the two buildings—remember? The one who made that shadow."

"I know. I heard his name then too. But what—?"

"But we're going to see to it that Anthony gets his signal, anyway," Ken explained. He showed Sandy the flashlight in his hand. "Then it won't be a wild-goose chase after all. Anthony will think he's in the clear, and he'll do whatever it is he's planning to do in that case."

"Great!" Sandy grinned. "And Thompson will be right behind him—Johnny on the spot!"

The second hand swept around twice more.

"Almost time," Ken said, when there were only ten seconds left to go. "Shield me from Jackson's dock."

Sandy stepped quickly to Ken's other side and opened his jacket wide. Within its protective cover Ken aimed the flashlight toward the inlet, waited until the second hand crossed the mark, and then blinked it three times.

"That's that," he said. "Now—"

"Ken!" Sandy grabbed his arm. "Those incoming ships—the ones arriving from Europe. I'll bet they've got something to do with all this! If Samson and Anthony keep tabs on them, and Thompson does too— Do you suppose somebody on board throws something overboard, and Jackson or Anthony catch it? Maybe they're a smuggling ring!"

"That's what I'm beginning to suspect too," Ken agreed. "I won't take your bet. But," he added, "how could you throw something overboard from a liner and expect it to be caught—or what it is you would risk throwing?" He shrugged. "Let's hope Thompson knows more about all this than we do."

"Shall we wake the Batesons?" Sandy asked excitedly.

"I guess we'd better." But Ken had already started to walk in the direction from which they'd come a few minutes before. "First, though—before it's too late—

let's check up on Jackson. If he leaves before he's supposed to we'll know he suspects something."

Sandy held him back. "Check—let's visit the Jackson dock right now. But by water."

"By water?"

"Sure. They'll be less likely to see us that way. We'll just grab a rowboat and drift by—silent like Indians."

Ken nodded. "Smart idea. Hope there are oars in the boat."

"There are," Sandy said a minute later as he jumped quietly into the small craft alongside the dock.

"All set?" Ken waited until he heard the oars slip into the locks, and then he let the rope fall into the boat and lowered himself into a bow seat. "When you get past Anthony's, cut close to shore so we can approach the *Sea Robin* from under Jackson's dock."

Sandy dug the oars in deep and pulled gently, veering to avoid the *Traveler* moored close by. After a dozen strokes he let the rowboat glide past the end of Anthony's dock, then pulled on his left oar and swung shoreward. A minute later he turned the boat again and headed straight for Jackson's dock. Just beyond it, the *Sea Robin's* mast showed up faintly against the sky.

Ken crouched on the seat, ready to grasp the piling, and fended the boat away from the barnacle-encrusted timbers. Carefully he edged the small craft in between two supports, and they were under the dock where the blackness was so intense as to be almost tangible.

When Ken had eased the boat out on the other side of the dock they were less than ten feet from the *Sea Robin's* stern.

Almost immediately heavy footsteps sounded overhead. Ken hurriedly pushed the rowboat back under the dock and both boys held their breath. Feet landed solidly on the *Sea Robin's* deck, followed by a resounding thud.

"Down below?" a voice asked.

"Yeah." It was Jackson who answered. "And snap it up. We have to carry the set out and get moving. Anthony can't keep him fooled all night, you know."

The hatch in the aft deck was dragged off and something thumped down into the shallow hold. Then the hatch was replaced and two sets of footsteps retreated shoreward.

"We've got to see what they put down below." Ken's whisper was barely audible. And he made no more noise as he vaulted over the low stern of the *Sea Robin*. He had the hatch part way up when Sandy landed beside him and lifted the heavy wooden cover clear.

Ken bent low, flashed his light inside the hold for a brief instant, and then straightened. "Lobsters—big ones, a basket full of them," he whispered against Sandy's ear.

They stared at each other for a moment in the faint reflected glow from the water. And then Sandy spoke.

"Hold the hatch up while I get rid of the boat." There was no mistaking the intensity of his gesture. Ken obeyed.

Sandy swung around and dropped the mooring line of the rowboat back into the tiny craft. Then he gave her a gentle nudge and she slid between the timbers, out of sight under the dock.

"Now—inside," he ordered. "Quick."

Ken gave him one last puzzled glance and then lowered himself into the *Sea Robin's* shallow aft hold, his shoulders supporting the heavy hatch. Sandy wriggled down beside him and let the cover softly into place.

"What's the idea?" Ken demanded then.

"Anthony's leading the *Dolphin* right to the scene of the action—but we forgot that Jackson'll be going there too. *With* that bruiser Burns. The odds are going to be pretty heavy against Thompson and his skipper."

In the absolute, close darkness of the hold each of them could hear his own heart thumping.

"You're right. I wasn't so smart," Ken said, after a long moment. "But what can we do about it—down here?"

"Well—" Sandy's voice had lost its positiveness. "I thought we'd at least be on hand—just in case. Unless you think— We can still get out."

Ken risked a quick stab of the flashlight. There was about three feet of headroom where they knelt, directly beneath the hatch, but on either side the space tapered away to less than two feet. In front of them, toward the cabin, and beyond an eighteen-inch timber brace was the engine. Beyond the engine was the opening in the bulkhead giving into the cabin.

"Leave these beautiful quarters?" There was a strained grin behind Ken's tone. "You must be crazy."

The deck overhead vibrated as someone jumped aboard. Two more similar thuds followed immediately.

"Flatten out," Ken breathed.

They crawled as far as they could to the portside of the hold. There wasn't enough room to kneel in the narrow space, but when they stretched out, trying to adjust their cramped bodies to the cross ribs of the hull, they felt certain they were invisible to anyone in the cabin who might cast a casual glance through the bulkhead opening.

The cabin door squeaked and feet descended the short ladder.

"Pull the curtains before you turn on the lights!"

"Right." Something heavy landed on the cabin floor and a moment later the lights came on.

From their hiding place the boys could see only the cabin's two lower bunks, a pair of rubber-booted legs, and a formidable piece of apparatus standing on the floor. It seemed to consist chiefly of dials and meters.

"Cut to the underwater exhaust." Jackson's voice grated from the deck.

The pair of boots approached the engine and a large hand groped around the machinery—apparently without success.

An instant later the head and shoulders of Plauk, Jackson's crewman, appeared in the bulkhead opening, and the beam of a flashlight vividly illuminated the shallow hold.

CHAPTER XVII

A PREMATURE SIGNAL

THE FLASHLIGHT slanted upward and then down, veered to right and left, and finally focused on a large valve. Plauk's big hand reached in and turned the handle, moved to another handle and turned it too. And as he worked he seemed to be staring intently at the rigid figures of Ken and Sandy, only a few feet beyond his finger tips.

Ken lay without breathing, trying to convince himself that they were invisible behind the low cross brace. While Plauk seemed to be looking directly at them—probably he could see nothing beyond the bright circle of light now steadily illuminating the *Sea Robin's* engine.

Probably, Ken reminded himself. There was no way of being certain. He could feel Sandy's tense body beside him, and the dampness in the bottom of the hold began to seep through his clothes.

Plauk's hand left the second valve, and groped toward them. Ken shivered. The hand came to rest on a spark plug wire, tested it, and then withdrew. Plauk swung the flashlight in one more exploratory circle and

—just as Ken felt it flick over his hunched shoulder—suddenly blacked it out. Ken shut his eyes for a brief instant, and when he opened them again Plauk was backing out of the little opening into the cabin beyond.

"O.K.," Plauk called quietly.

The *Sea Robin's* engine was grinding before Ken permitted himself to breathe.

Three of the cylinders coughed alive first, but a moment later all had settled down to a steady rumble. Suddenly Plauk bent down again, cast his light over the engine once more, felt the block, and nodded soberly to himself. This time when he backed out and stood up he disappeared completely out of the line of their vision. An instant later the cabin light blacked out.

The engine speeded up, subsided, and then quickened again. The whole boat shook with its motion, and the tiny hold was filled with vibrating sound. The planking creaked, and they were aware of the water moving swiftly under the floor of the hold.

Ken sighed his relief, and moved a cramped muscle.

"Close call," Sandy muttered under the noise of the engine.

"Too close," Ken agreed. "Underwater exhaust," he added a moment later. "No wonder he's been able to sneak out at night."

The boat heeled, and the timbers complained loudly as she was put about. All the water in the bilge sloshed over to the side where they lay.

"Slightly damp in here," Sandy commented. "Think we ought to complain?"

"Wouldn't do any good. We've signed on for the duration."

The *Sea Robin* heeled over again, and once more the bilge water sloshed over them. Then the motion of the boat changed—she began to rise and fall steadily, and the engine speeded up again.

"Must be out in the bay," Ken said. He was speaking in a normal tone, but even so he had to put his mouth almost against Sandy's ear to be heard in the noisily echoing hold.

Sandy's answer was a cough, and a moment later Ken was coughing too. The small space was filling rapidly with the reek of gasoline and hot oil—a reek that caught sharply at the throat. Ken covered the flashlight with one hand and turned it on. The tiny ray he allowed to escape looked like a thin white thread hanging in the haze of smoke. Ken turned the light off and buried his face in the crook of his arm, fighting for breath.

"We can't take much of this," Sandy gasped. "Think we could lift the hatch a little?"

Ken had to wait until a fit of coughing had passed before he could answer. "Too risky," he said then. "Engine would sound different."

"But we—"

"Breathe—through—your—handkerchief." The words were half lost in the coughing that accompanied them, but as Ken wriggled onto one side to reach into his pocket Sandy caught the idea too.

Together they pulled out their handkerchiefs, soaked them in bilge water, and pressed the wet cloth against their faces.

But the *Sea Robin* was traveling steadily now, and as the minutes went by, the engine grew hotter and the fumes more insistent.

The boys lay still, breathing shallowly, their faces so close to the planking that they were intermittently washed by the bilge.

Ken found himself fighting the impulse to crawl boldly out into the cabin, while he still had the strength to move. Even Plauk and Jackson and Burns began to seem less dangerous than certain asphyxiation.

Suddenly the cabin door squeaked open and slammed shut again, and the cabin light came on. Two pairs of legs appeared beside the dial-encrusted apparatus on the floor. One pair was encased in rubber boots, the other in dark trousers and ordinary shoes.

Ken muffled a cough desperately in his handkerchief: the two figures were so close that they might be able to hear a strange sound even through the noise of the engine.

"This place smells like a garage!" It was Burns's irritable voice that spoke. "Can't you do something about it?"

"Keep your shirt on," Jackson growled back. "Can't have a boat engine without fumes."

"But this—" Burns broke off in a fit of coughing.

"All right—all right." Jackson sounded impatient. "I'll do something about 'em."

The light went out again and the cabin door was opened.

"Plauk!" Jackson called brusquely through the doorway. "Open the hatch a couple of inches. Mr. Burns here likes fresh air." He closed the door and turned on the light again.

Ken grinned weakly to himself, and held back a cough by one last effort of will. He wondered how

Burns would enjoy knowing that he had probably saved their lives.

Overhead the hatch scraped as it was slid open, and a strong air current swept over their water-soaked figures. Ken and Sandy both lifted their heads to suck in great draughts of it, and within less than a minute they had stuffed their handkerchiefs back in their pockets and were able to breathe almost normally again. The steady surge of air now swooping past them chilled their skin, but any degree of cold was preferable to the painful fumes they had just experienced.

Ken twisted around. Sandy's head was only a foot from his, but it was entirely invisible in the darkness. Ken reassured himself that they couldn't possibly be seen from the lighted cabin. Both the boys settled themselves as comfortably as possible, in positions that permitted them to watch whatever might be seen through the bulkhead opening.

Burns and Jackson had seated themselves on the lower bunks and were bending forward, bringing their heads within range. Burns—there was no doubt now that he was one of the men they had seen in the office over the Live Lobster—was lighting a cigarette. He dropped the match on the floor.

"Cut that out!" Jackson stamped on the match, then picked it up and dropped it in a coffee can at the foot of the bunk. "There's too much gasoline around here to play with matches!"

Burns shrugged his shoulders and spoke briefly, but his words were inaudible over the noise of the engine.

Jackson got to his feet and reached for something on

the upper starboard bunk. When he set it down on the floor the boys could see that it was a small kerosene lantern. Jackson lighted it and ostentatiously put the match in the coffee can. Then he clamped the lantern to one of the bunks, and its single small beam of light struck directly at the top of the apparatus at his feet.

Jackson knelt on the cabin floor, opened a door in the side of the mechanism, and removed a disk and a device resembling a big doughnut on the end of a short stick.

Sandy put his mouth up against Ken's ear. "Radio direction finder," he whispered. "The disk is a compass. That other thing is the antenna."

Jackson had set the compass card on top of the radio apparatus and inserted the antenna through the card into a socket in the set. Now he was attaching some wires to binding posts, talking to Burns over his shoulder as he worked.

Burns nodded, apparently at the explanation Jackson had given, and then leaned forward to swing the circular antenna around. Jackson nodded.

Then the lobster pirate looked up suddenly and turned off the light. With the kerosene lantern left as the only illumination in the cabin, little was visible except the top of the radio compass, its white card bright in the beam of light.

The cabin door squealed as Jackson slid it open. "What?"

Plauk's voice sounded from the deck. "I said she's in sight—about four miles offshore."

"O.K. I'm coming up," Jackson told him.

The cabin door banged shut behind him.

Burns lighted another cigarette, this time depositing the match in the can, and settled back on the bunk as if he expected to remain there indefinitely.

"What's 'in sight—about four miles offshore'?" Sandy's whisper barely carried the inch to Ken's ear. "An incoming liner?"

"Sounds likely," Ken agreed.

"Be easy to ruin that radio finder."

"Be easier for Burns to put us out of commission as we crawl out of here," Ken pointed out.

The rudder cables moved and the boat heeled as she turned hard to starboard. Almost immediately the motion changed a second time. Now the *Sea Robin* was rising and falling much more heavily, and the water in the bilge washed back and forth over their prone figures.

Suddenly Burns hauled himself erect on the bunk, his face a pale greenish blur in the outer glow of the small light. He grasped the corner support and started to his feet, striking his head hard against the upper bunk. For a moment he sank back again and then, one hand to his head, staggered up off the bunk and lunged unsteadily toward the door.

Jackson came down the ladder before Burns could reach it. He flicked on the light as he closed the door, and pushed Burns back toward the bunk. For an instant he grinned down at him, and then he settled himself on the floor and turned on the direction finder. He checked the dials and finally slipped a pair of headphones over his ears.

For a moment he listened intently, before he hung the phones back on their hook and shut the set off. He left the cabin again after one more derisive look at Burns, switching off the light before he opened the door.

"Maybe we could rush Burns," Sandy whispered. "He looks sick enough to be a pushover."

"And then what?" When Sandy didn't answer, Ken continued, "No—it's too early yet to ask for trouble. We can always ruin the engine if things get too bad."

"O.K." Sandy moved slightly to ease his cramped shoulders. "This is a bad place to be caught—no chance to fight."

The boat's pitching eased off as she moved out into the open sea and after a while Burns stood up again, carefully ducking to avoid the upper bunk this time. Jackson dropped back into the cabin just as he straightened up, and simultaneously the engine gained speed. The vibration increased and the noise grew louder.

Jackson pointed to his watch and said something to Burns, who shrugged and sat heavily down on the bunk again. Jackson poured himself a cup of coffee from a thermos bottle, sitting on the edge of the opposite bunk to drink it. Burns closed his eyes.

For fifteen minutes the boat raced on, its engine shaking with the effort it was putting forth. Then without warning it throttled down to idling speed. The relative silence was overwhelming.

Jackson got to his feet. "In position?" he called.

"Just about," Plauk called down. "We're on, but it'll take her five minutes to make the point."

Jackson pulled a long tubelike affair from under the bunk and handed it up through the doorway to Plauk. "You give the signal when she's there." He settled on the floor again and turned on the radio finder. "Better get this thing warmed up."

Burns, looking less ill now that the boat had quieted down, leaned forward to inspect the apparatus more closely. "Never did know how you manage your end of it," he said. "How do they know where to dump it, anyway?"

Jackson slid the earphones forward onto his cheeks so that he could hear. "Huh?"

Burns repeated the question.

"Easy," Jackson told him. "There are two buoys off here, marking some shoals. When the ship is in line with those two lights, we give the signal and he answers. Then he chucks it overboard. If he doesn't get the signal, he doesn't throw. After it's in the water, of course, we pick it up with this baby"—he gestured toward the direction finder—"and I guess you know the rest of it."

"Yeah." Burns nodded. "Pretty slick. Wouldn't think you could ever find anything out here in the dark, though."

"There's a little bell on it," Jackson explained. "The finder gets us close enough to hear the bell. The rest is up to us."

"Hey!" There was a note of panic in Plauk's sudden shout.

"What's the matter with you?" Jackson had leaped to his feet and was speaking through the door. "Keep your voice down. Want to advertise us all over the Atlantic?"

"Come up here! There's something wrong!" Plauk's voice was more subdued, but it had lost none of its urgency.

Jackson yanked the door open and landed on deck.

Burns, starting up to go after him, forgot the bunk above him again and crashed against the hard wood with a resounding thump. He fell back, rocked for a moment with his head in his hands, and then eased himself erect and staggered up the ladder.

"What's wrong?" Jackson's voice was filtering faintly through the opened hatch. "Didn't you get the answering signal?"

"I got it—I got it before I sent our signal!"

"Huh?" It was a bewildered grunt. "How could you?" Jackson demanded.

"Somebody must have signaled." Burns was suddenly taking command. "Somebody got here ahead of us."

"But who? Anthony's the only one who knows our signals—and *he's* not here," Jackson pointed out.

"If it is Anthony—if he's trying to double-cross us—" Burns began.

"He wouldn't come this way—not with a government boat on his stern," Jackson growled. "Unless—" he stopped.

"Unless what?"

"Unless the government boat picked him up and made him talk."

The *Sea Robin's* engine began to roar again, and just as suddenly was cut back to idling speed.

"What do you think you're doing?" Burns demanded.

"We're getting out of here while the getting is good."

"No, you're not, Jackson. Not while I've got this thing in my hand." Burns sounded vicious. "There's two hundred thousand dollars worth of diamonds coming off that ship and we're picking them up. Understand?"

CHAPTER XVIII

"RAM HER AMIDSHIPS!"

THE SILENCE that followed Burns's words seemed to go
on endlessly. There wasn't even a footfall on the deck
over the boys' heads to denote any kind of motion. Only
the engine stayed alive, ticking over slowly and quietly.

"Burns must have pulled a gun," Sandy breathed
against Ken's ear. "If they get into a fight—"

The deck timbers creaked suddenly; someone had
moved.

"Stay where you are!" Burns barked.

"Don't be a fool." If Jackson had been momentarily
alarmed he seemed calm enough now. His voice suggested only scornful irritation. "You can't make us do
anything—because you can't run a boat. If anything
happened to us you'd have to jump overboard and swim
back. You'd never get ashore any other way."

"*You* won't get back at all," Burns answered.

"O.K." Jackson laughed. "Looks like this is a stale-
mate."

Plauk took a hand. "Look, Burns, let's not blow our
tops. If the customs men did pick up Anthony, we'd

better make tracks. Nothing we can do around here in that case. Be smarter to warn the rest and give them a chance to get away."

"All they've got to do is catch a glimpse of one of us acting any way suspicious out here," Jackson took it up. "Even if they haven't got Anthony—or if they've got him and he hasn't talked—they'll still know enough to make it hot for us. You say they've already been snooping around the restaurant."

"Well, yeah—but wait a minute. We can't even be sure that something's gone wrong yet. Maybe that signal got flashed by accident." Burns was shifting his tactics from force to persuasion. "I don't want to put my head in a noose any more than you do. But what harm will it do for us to stick around here awhile? This is a quiet boat, with the underwater exhaust. Why don't we get a sight on the tube with the direction finder, and just edge up on her? We can fade out again if anybody's got there ahead of us."

"Makes sense," Plauk said, after a short silence.

"Except for that gun." Jackson had capitulated too. "I don't like guns when they're pointed at me."

"Oh—sorry." Burns laughed. "Guess I lost my head for a minute. Now." He sounded authoritative again. "What do we do?"

"We go below and turn on the finder. Plauk, I'll give you the course as usual. Keep her throttled down."

"Right."

Back in the cabin, Jackson clamped the earphones over his head and began to swing the antenna back and forth in slow sweeps. Burns sat on the bunk, leaning forward intently, watching every move.

Jackson stopped the antenna's motion abruptly, moved it back an inch, and then reversed it again. He steadied it after another few seconds of careful manipulation, bent low to check the compass card, and then called softly up to Plauk. "East two points."

"Right." The rudder cable rumbled through its pulleys and the boat swung slightly.

Jackson moved the antenna to compensate for the change in the *Sea Robin's* course. The antenna was pointing almost directly at the bow. "East one point."

"One point. Right."

Again the boat swung slightly, and once more Jackson shifted the radio finder antenna.

"Steady as she is." Jackson slipped the phones off his head and stood up. "We're heading right for it. Let's go on deck and see what we can see. Keep your voice down up there now."

"Don't worry about me. See that you and Plauk remember that."

Sandy leaned close to Ken. "If they're going to stay up there, this would be a good chance to—"

"That wouldn't help now. They've got their course. But let's shift back a little so we can be sure to hear through the hatchway."

Slowly, stiff with wet and cold, they began to ease their bodies backward. The hatch cover had been slid back almost a foot, and when their heads were beneath the opening they could look straight up into the star-studded sky.

Cautiously Ken lifted himself until his eyes were on a level with the deck. He cast a hasty look around before he lowered himself again. The darkness had been complete. The *Sea Robin* was entirely blacked out.

"Now," Jackson was saying, "all we can do is wait."

"How much farther?" Burns wanted to know.

"Straight ahead about a mile." The engine slowed down even more. "From here on we'll take it mighty easy."

For a long five minutes, then, there was no further talk on deck. The *Sea Robin's* forward motion was slight, her engine turning over so slowly that the gurgle of the exhaust was hardly audible.

At the end of that period Ken raised his head once more to peer out over the edge of the hatchway. Cautiously Sandy joined him. After the darkness of the hold the starlit night seemed almost bright, and soon they were able to make out the three figures grouped closely around the wheel, their heads and shoulders silhouetted against the dim shape of the windshield.

As they watched, the central figure moved. A rasping noise cut the silence. A match flared.

The sharp sound of a slap punctuated the incident. The match had been extinguished.

"You fool!" There was fury in Jackson's harsh whisper. "Don't you know you can see the light of a match for miles out here—on a night like this?"

"Who do you think you're—?"

"Cut it out, you two!" Plauk snapped quietly. "We've got enough trouble as it is."

"For two cents I'd dump him overboard," Jackson muttered.

"You—and how many other bungling—?"

"Cut it out!" Plauk repeated.

This time they heeded his tense command. Standing a little apart now, all three men remained silent as the *Sea Robin* moved slowly and quietly ahead.

"I'll go down and check," Jackson murmured finally. "I can tell if the tube's still afloat."

The boys ducked their heads down and craned forward to look past the engine into the cabin. Jackson was operating the antenna again. In the dim light from the lantern his face took on a puzzled expression.

"Still getting it?" Plauk asked quietly from the doorway.

"Yeah—but it's shifted. Or we have."

"We're still on the course," Plauk protested.

Jackson shook his head, listening intently, and then looked up toward the doorway. "South three points," he ordered.

"Right."

The loop antenna under Jackson's manipulation was moving again. "South one point."

"Right."

Jackson rubbed a big hand over his stubbled jaw. "South one point."

"Again? You just said—"

"Yes—again!" Jackson glared at the antenna and then up toward the doorway. "Something's fishy here. The tube's moving. It's on a boat, or—"

"Come up here!" Plauk's sudden demand cut him short.

Jackson ripped the earphones off and lunged for the ladder.

In their cramped quarters the boys wriggled around

until they were able to peer through the hatchway again.

Ken blinked. No longer were the stars the only visible light. There was a curious faint glow low on the horizon now, dead ahead of the *Sea Robin*. Against it the bulking shapes of Jackson, Plauk, and Burns were sharply outlined.

Jackson, his long arms braced, was on the portside, leaning out beyond the windshield. Burns had climbed up on the cabin roof, where he crouched alongside the mast. Plauk kept his hold on the wheel, but he too was leaning forward.

Jackson turned around, saw Burns, and motioned to him to come back down on the deck. After a moment Burns obeyed.

"What's going on?" Burns asked. There was no longer a trace of bluster in his low, panicky voice.

"Plenty." Jackson spoke so quietly that the boys could barely make out what he said. "That's Anthony's boat out there—caught in the *Dolphin's* searchlight."

"What?" Burns's voice rose in a squeak, and Jackson's hand lowered warningly on his arm.

"That's right. Sure you don't know anything about this? You were in charge of the signals—you knew what they were."

"But I was only supposed to signal him if the *Dolphin* didn't follow him—and it did. Why should I—?"

"But nobody else knew about the signals." Jackson's whisper was menacing, and he was still holding Burns's arm. "He was supposed to decide on 'em just before he left."

"He did! Nobody knew! He—" Burns stopped, as if

suddenly aware that he was incriminating himself. "But somebody must have found out. Unless Anthony—"

"He wouldn't have come out here on his own—with a customs man right behind him—unless somebody crossed him up." Jackson flung Burns aside and spoke to Plauk. "Let's get out of here!"

"But wait!" Frantically Burns thrust himself between the two men. "There's a quarter of a million bucks worth—"

"Nothing doing!" Jackson's long arm encircled Burns, lifted him off the deck, and set him down again several feet away. With his other hand he reached for the throttle. "Put her over, Plauk."

"But listen to me—just *listen* a minute!" When Jackson turned toward him again Burns put out his hands to ward off the menacing figure, but without pausing in his hurried whisper. "If they get Anthony they'll get all of us! Our only chance now is to get Anthony away from them. Don't you—?"

Jackson deliberately turned his back on him and bent over the wheel.

"Don't you see?" Burns went on desperately. "Listen: this boat's quiet. They're busy—they won't even notice us if we come up easy—from behind, like this. What would happen if we crashed right into the *Dolphin?*"

Jackson didn't answer, but there was a rigidity to his back that suggested he was finally listening to Burns.

"It would be an accident—see?" Burns added.

Jackson spoke over his shoulder without turning around. "An accident to the *Sea Robin,* you mean. And that means us."

"Sure!" Burns's voice had suddenly gained confidence. "That's right. But more of an accident for the *Dolphin*. The *Dolphin* would go down fast—she's light, built for speed. She'd go down with all hands. Get it? Lost at sea and no questions asked."

"He's got something there." Plauk's thoughtful voice cut in. "We could cut her in half like cheese. And drowned men don't talk."

"That's the idea!" Burns edged up close to them, but he spoke more coolly now, sure of Plauk's support. "If the *Sea Robin* gets hurt, we buy you a new boat out of the profits."

He paused a moment. "But we've got to act fast," he said then in a tone of command. "Don't want to wait until the *Dolphin's* got the stones aboard."

"O.K." Jackson's surrender had been clear before he admitted it. He opened the throttle, and at the same moment picked up a pair of glasses to peer ahead toward that glow. "They're about five hundred feet apart yet," he reported, "but the *Dolphin's* closing in fast. Anthony's on his aft deck—with his hands up."

Anthony's plight seemed to make Jackson more decisive. He spoke to Plauk without turning his head. "Put her back a little—we're going too fast."

The *Sea Robin* slowed obediently.

"But we've *got* to go fast!" Burns said. "If you—"

"Let me handle this," Jackson interrupted. "If we get within two hundred feet of the *Dolphin* without them sighting us, we'll be O.K. It'll take half a minute more from that point—not enough time for them to get out of the way. We'll hit the *Dolphin* amidships."

"Well—"

"I'm telling you." Jackson made it clear that there

would be no further discussion. "I'll take the wheel, Plauk," he went on. "You go below and get—"

His last words were inaudible to the boys. Plauk disappeared briefly and when he returned he had three life preservers in his arms. He gave one to Burns and one to Jackson and slipped the third one on.

"We jump when we're a hundred feet off," Jackson ordered.

"And jump wide," Plauk cautioned Burns.

"Right," Jackson agreed. "I'll open her up just before we go over, and you want to make sure you stay clear of the propeller."

"Maybe it would be safe to stay aboard." Burns sounded nervous. "You really think the *Sea Robin* will go down too? After all, she's pretty heavy. Maybe we—"

"She'll go—the way I'm aimin' to ram the *Dolphin*." Jackson seemed to take a grim pleasure in Burns's fright. "This was your idea, remember. The *Sea Robin*'ll sink in about a minute flat."

Plauk moved to the rail. "Come on, Burns—get ready."

"We jump in about two minutes," Jackson warned. "You set?"

"Sure," Plauk said quietly. "I've got a flash to signal Anthony with."

The boys sank back into the hold. "About a minute left," Ken whispered, "before Thompson and Jones—"

"Before Holt and Allen," Sandy cut in, "get caught like the well-known rats in the well-known trap."

CHAPTER XIX

HEADED FOR THE ROCKS

THE ENGINE ticked on—counting off the precious seconds that remained. Sandy began to raise his head. "We'd better get out of this hold before she hits."

"Not yet!" Ken pulled him back. "We wouldn't last a minute if they caught sight of us."

"That valve—the one that switches on the underwater exhaust!" Sandy was clutching Ken's arm. "We'll shift it back and let the exhaust go! Thompson would hear."

"No time. We're going up on deck—but we've got to do it right. You take Burns and Plauk; I'll take Jackson. Throw them over if you have to—but don't jump yourself."

"What—?"

Ken cut the discussion short by raising his head up through the hatchway. He made room for Sandy beside him.

The glow of light beyond the bow was brighter than it had been before. Plauk and Burns were still at the rail, Jackson was still at the wheel.

Ken slid the hatch cover back an inch. It didn't creak. He moved it again and then once more. It was almost halfway open now. The next time he shoved it he had forced an opening wide enough for them to crawl through.

"Ready!" Jackson's order was low and tense. He moved the wheel and the boat swung slightly to starboard. "I'll count to three. Jump on three."

"Right."

Ken spoke against Sandy's ear. "We go on two."

"One!" Jackson said.

Ken could feel Sandy's muscles tighten. The big redhead had his hands on the rim of the hatchway—he was measuring the distance between himself and the two figures at the rail.

"Two!"

Sandy cleared the hatchway silently and then launched his two hundred pounds forward in a rush. That much Ken saw before he himself leaped up and out and tore for his target at the wheel.

"Three!" The command was a triumphant shout.

As he spoke Jackson shoved the throttle to full speed, and in the same instant turned toward the starboard rail. Even as he spun, the *Sea Robin* leaped forward, her bow coming up with the force of her new speed.

Ken hit him as he took his second step. His shoulder struck the burly figure's side and lifted it off the deck. There was no time to follow up. As one of Ken's hands reached frantically for the throttle, the other grabbed at the wheel. His eyes tried to take in the entire scene at one quick sweep.

The *Dolphin* lay directly in front of them, across the

Sea Robin's bow. Her searchlight still flooded the deck of the all-but-overtaken *Stingray*. In the forward cock-pit of the government boat, lighted to his waist by the beam of light, stood Thompson. A submachine gun was cradled in his arm.

He had heard the oncoming boat—there was no doubt of that. When Ken first sighted him he was swinging toward it, his mouth wide with surprise.

Ken's fingers closed on the wheel, yanked to star-board, then slipped off. The *Sea Robin's* bow had veered a little. It pointed to the *Dolphin's* forward cockpit now instead of dead amidships. But there was only a hundred feet between the two boats.

Ken gripped the spokes again and pulled desperately. The hundred feet had shrunk to eighty.

He heard a bellow from behind him—a roar of rage. But he hung on the wheel. The bow was coming around now. Already it was pointing at the *Dolphin's* bow. There was only fifty feet between them.

Something struck the back of Ken's neck. His head bounced against the windshield and rocked back. Some-thing tore at the wheel—pulled it to port. A smashing blow struck at his own hands on the spokes.

Ken hung on, his fingers numb, fighting a vaster numbness that seemed to be creeping down from his neck.

Thirty feet.

The wheel jerked hard to port, against all the force Ken could muster. The *Sea Robin's* bow swung sharply back, to aim at the *Dolphin's* center. Ken gritted his teeth and threw every ounce of his weight into an effort to drag the wheel over again. But his weight wasn't enough. The wheel held. The pressure on his side and back was gradually forcing him off balance.

Then suddenly the pressure dissolved, and the wheel swung freely. Ken almost went to his knees as it spun full to starboard. The *Sea Robin* careened wildly.

Her bow cleared the *Dolphin* by inches. Her stern almost scraped the low black boat, and her rolling wash lifted the lighter craft like an empty tin can.

Ken hung onto the wheel. After the *Dolphin* was astern he shook his head to clear it, and his eyes began to focus again. He risked a swift glance around.

A half cry stuck somewhere in his throat.

Anthony had taken advantage of the confusion to make a break for freedom. The *Stingray* had leaped forward under full throttle. Already she was charging ahead of the *Dolphin* at top speed, the water cascading away from her raised bow. The angle at which she was traveling, and the curving course of the *Sea Robin,* would force a collision on the *Sea Robin's* portside.

"Jump!" Ken found himself shouting. "Sandy! Jump!" He was still pulling uselessly on the wheel.

The searchlight of the *Dolphin* highlighted the *Stingray's* sharp bow, making it gleam like a knife. It dipped into a trough and rose high on the next wave, terrifyingly near. Only a single trough separated her from the *Sea Robin* now. When she dipped into it—

Time seemed to stand still while the *Stingray* hung poised atop that wall of water. Instinctively Ken flung an arm halfway across his face. The *Stingray's* bow dipped, slowly at first, and then faster.

But suddenly the oncoming bow veered and dug itself into a swell a foot from the *Sea Robin's* side.

Ken scarcely felt the water that cascaded over the rail and flung him backward, hand still clinging to the wheel.

The *Stingray* was swinging hard to port now, its starboard rail almost under with the force of its swerve.

In the darkness—the *Dolphin's* searchlight had lost its careening target—the bumpers of the two boats touched and bounced apart.

An unidentifiable voice shouted urgently across the space between them. "Take this!" Something flashed briefly and landed with a hollow thump on the *Sea Robin's* deck. "Get to shore! We'll cover up!"

A new small beam of light, from the same source as the voice, hit Ken directly, disappeared, and then flashed on.

When the voice from the *Stingray* shouted again it was a bellow of rage. "Holt! Where's—?"

Almost in the instant that the light disappeared, a figure hurled itself across the six feet of water between the two boats. Ken didn't realize what had happened until he felt something heavy land hard on the deck beside him. He took his hands off the wheel and spun around.

Anthony was already hauling himself erect from the sprawl in which he had landed. In the same moment that Ken recognized him he also saw the small ugly automatic glinting in Anthony's hand.

"Where's Jackson? Where's Burns?" Anthony's voice was a breathless gasp, and when he took a step forward he staggered and had to steady himself against the cabin. "What are *you* doing here?"

Ken saw him fight for his balance again as the *Sea*

Robin, plunging erratically out to sea, dipped her bow. He seized the split-second's respite to scan the deck.

Where was Sandy?

The *Dolphin,* some distance behind now, was once again training its powerful flash on the wallowing *Stingray,* planted squarely across her bow in an obvious attempt to halt the *Dolphin's* progress. There was no light at all on the *Sea Robin*—Ken could barely recognize Anthony at the distance of a few feet. But if Sandy were still aboard, he— Had he jumped? Had they all jumped?

Suddenly Ken remembered his silent battle over the wheel, and its abrupt ending. That had been Jackson, he realized now. And it must have been Sandy who hauled him away. They must have gone overboard then —both of them.

But Jackson had a life preserver—and Sandy didn't.

And Sandy didn't swim very well.

Ken grabbed the wheel and hauled it over hard. The *Sea Robin* swung to port with a sickening lurch. His left hand groped over the panel where the searchlight switch should be.

Something hard drove against his spine. The wheel was torn out of his hands and reversed. The *Sea Robin* swayed from side to side as the rudder came over.

"This is a gun in your back." Anthony's voice was steady now and menacingly cold. "Don't make me use it."

Ken ignored the warning. There was only a single thought in his head. "He's overboard!" He grabbed at the wheel again. "Got to turn back! He—"

"Don't move. Take your hands off that wheel! Right

now I don't care if Jackson does drown—or Burns or Plauk either."

For an instant Ken didn't understand. And then he realized that Anthony thought he had referred to one of his own three men. Anthony didn't know about Sandy.

"But I—" Ken began, and stopped. There was no time for argument.

He would chance it. He couldn't leave Sandy out there.

"Don't be a fool!" Anthony barked as Ken's muscles tensed for a leap. "I said don't move—and I mean it."

He did mean it. It was impossible to doubt the determination behind that voice, or behind the gun barrel that was still boring a hole in Ken's back.

Ken knew the trigger would be pulled instantly unless he obeyed.

He held himself still, and despair flooded over him.

"O.K." Anthony had sensed his capitulation. "Get your hands clear of the wheel and move aside."

Dully Ken obeyed. He turned slowly and slumped back against the cabin wall. Anthony maneuvered the wheel with one hand—the other kept the gun steadily pointed.

Far behind—more than a mile astern by now—the *Dolphin's* light still held the *Stingray* pinned to the dark water. The two boats were very close together.

As Ken watched, a second searchlight flared into life on the *Dolphin*, pointed skyward for an instant and then dipped down and swept the sea in great arcs.

Anthony laughed softly. "Good—the government to the rescue. That ought to keep the *Dolphin* occupied for half an hour, anyway. Gives us plenty of time to get away from here." He flipped on the binnacle light and checked the compass, keeping one wary eye on Ken. When he had swung the wheel a quarter turn and pulled it back again, he slipped a loop over it to hold it in position.

"O.K.," he said then. "Get down inside the cabin." His carefully shaded flash illuminated the doorway.

Ken moved slowly toward it, his eyes still on the searchlight playing over the distant water. Sandy would be picked up, he told himself—probably he was already safe aboard the *Dolphin*. He *must* be.

"Hurry up!" Anthony ordered.

Ken stumbled down the three steps into the little cabin.

"Sit there." The small spot of light indicated the bottom step. "Where I can keep an eye on you."

Sandy *had* to be all right, Ken again reassured himself. He was on board the *Dolphin*—of course he was. Right this minute, in fact, he was probably telling Thompson everything they had learned during this hectic night, explaining to the customs man that Vic Samson and Anthony and—

Ken's thoughts stopped dead. What could Sandy be telling him about Anthony? He didn't know—probably nobody knew—that Anthony was now on the *Sea Robin*, heading swiftly out of the *Dolphin's* range.

"You'll never get away from them," Ken heard himself saying aloud. "The *Dolphin's* got radar aboard. She can overhaul you in no time."

But even as he spoke he knew he was trying to convince himself as much as Anthony. And he knew, too, that it hadn't worked.

"You let me worry about that," Anthony said. He'd set his flashlight alongside the compass, so that its beam held steadily on Ken. "You just sit there."

His voice faded on the last word and Ken swung around—too late. Anthony had turned away for a second, but as Ken focused on his shadowy figure it was watchfully facing him again, the gun still ominously present.

But now Anthony had a strange object in his other hand—a long gleaming cylinder. It tinkled like a bell each time it moved. An instant later Ken recognized it as a replica of the "stovepipe" Sandy's flash picture had caught. This one, he realized, was what Anthony had thrown over to the *Sea Robin's* deck just before he had jumped.

The cylinder was only about three inches in diameter and two feet long, with a slender flexible rod extending a foot from one end. Anthony had clamped the tube between his knees and with his one free hand was unscrewing the end with the projecting rod. A moment later the lidlike cap was free, and Ken could see that there was a box-shaped contraption attached to its underside.

Anthony looked at it briefly before he tossed it overboard, the little bell ringing merrily until it sank.

Ken gasped.

"You guessed it—a radio transmitter." There was a grim amusement in Anthony's voice. "Don't want to keep it around. Might help the *Dolphin* to find us."

"She won't need any help." Ken did his best to put conviction into his voice. "They probably know exactly where we are right now."

"I'm sure they do—not that it'll do them any good. Or you either," Anthony added as he turned the cylinder upside down and caught the small chamois bag that dropped out.

The cylinder fell to the deck as Anthony unrolled and opened the soft leather sack. A moment later he deliberately held his hand in the flashlight's beam to show Ken the dozen brilliantly shining stones in his palm. When he spoke his voice was as hard as the diamonds themselves.

"You can understand," Anthony said, "why I can't afford to take any risks."

Carefully, then, he put the stones back into their bag, closed it and rerolled it, and tucked the bag securely into an inner pocket.

"Now," he said briskly, and the *Sea Robin* shifted her course as he put his hand to the wheel. "Open the locker under the port bunk and bring me a life preserver."

The beam of the flashlight and the muzzle of the gun followed Ken across the cabin. Obediently he bent down and opened the locker door, pulled out the last remaining life jacket. What were Anthony's plans, he wondered.

Was he—Ken felt a sudden surge of hope at the thought—was Anthony planning to jump overboard? Ken rebelled fiercely at the possibility that Anthony might thus get away with his haul of smuggled gems, but Anthony was a dangerous customer. So long as he remained aboard, at the other end of that very business-like gun, Ken knew that his own life hung by a slender thread. If, for any reason, he appeared to Anthony as a risk— Ken's jaws clenched. Anthony had already made it clear that he couldn't afford risks.

He handed the vestlike canvas garment up to the figure at the wheel. "Sit down on the steps again," Anthony said, and when Ken had obeyed he deftly fastened himself into the jacket without ever permitting the gun's aim to falter.

Then Anthony shifted course again and Ken felt a change in the motion of the boat. It was moving up and down now, cutting across the swells, the bow raising and then plunging heavily. But a few moments ago—

"What are you doing here, anyway?" Anthony's voice broke into his speculations. "How'd you get aboard?"

Ken waited a split second before he answered. The less he appeared to know, the less danger Anthony would think him.

"Trying to catch Jackson pirating lobsters," he said briefly.

Anthony snorted. "I thought so. I had 'em all fooled," he added, as if to himself.

"So you were looking for lobster pirates, huh?" Anthony laughed. "Almost found them, didn't you—with that picture. Too bad I spoiled it."

"You didn't," Ken said. "Sandy fooled *you*. He developed it and it came out fine."

Anthony was quite obviously jolted. "Where is it? And where is your friend?" He emphasized his question by bringing the gun closer.

Ken turned to look up at the man but said nothing.

Anthony backed away. "I get it—he's overboard—with my men. But where's that picture?"

Ken turned his back on his questioner.

Anthony laughed again. "I don't know what I'm worried about. The picture—if it is good—will show Jackson and Plauk—not me." He looked at the compass again before he went on. "I don't know how much you *do* know about this. But I really don't care."

The *Sea Robin* plunged and lifted again. Ken looked at his watch: fifteen minutes had elapsed since Anthony had leaped from the *Stingray*. When Anthony had first shifted course, the *Sea Robin* had ceased to roll sideways and had taken on a corkscrew motion, half bucking, half rolling. That meant Anthony must have headed her at an angle toward the headland. But now she was bucking up and down, heading across the swells.

Ken stiffened. She couldn't be! They couldn't have reached the headland in fifteen minutes. To head for shore now was suicide! Ted had said there were rocks there.

There was a curious scraping sound on deck. Ken half got to his feet to look out; the hatchway cover was closed—tight. Anthony had just kicked it shut.

"Sit down!" Anthony commanded, jabbing the gun toward Ken's face.

Ken's pulse was racing now—racing faster than the throbbing engine. Anthony's plan had suddenly become clear to him—clear and deadly.

Anthony was wearing the only life preserver. He was aiming for the rocks—deliberately—and he meant to jump to safety before the *Sea Robin* piled up. Ken would be left on board, probably locked in the cabin. The hatchway had been closed to shut off his escape by that route. And by the time Ken had managed to break out of the cabin . . .

In less than fifteen minutes now they'd near the shore. In less than a quarter of an hour . . .

Ken looked up at Anthony and then looked down again. The wild hope that he could somehow surprise and overpower his captor died in that single second. Anthony was far too wary to be taken by surprise. And Ken had no doubt that he would use his gun without an instant's hesitation.

The second hand on Ken's watch swept relentlessly around.

There was only one other hope. If he could somehow stop the engine—

Ken gripped the unyielding wood of the step he was seated on. The *Sea Robin's* engine was behind that bulkhead opening, almost within reach of his hand. But it might as well have been a hundred miles away. The first move he made toward it would produce an instant —and fatal—move on Anthony's part. The slightest pull of his trigger finger . . .

Ken looked at his watch once more. Another three minutes had gone by.

CHAPTER XX

FOG TO THE RESCUE

THE SECOND HAND made two more circuits of its dial as Ken watched it helplessly.

Suddenly, above him on deck, Anthony closed the throttle and threw the clutch out for an instant. The engine subsided to a low purr.

Ken twisted around awkwardly to look up at him. Then, slowly, he turned back again. He had heard something. It had sounded like a groan. And it had come from the hold—near the engine, or in back of it where he and Sandy had hidden themselves before. There it was again.

Ken ducked sideways, risking a swift glance through the small opening into the hold. It was too dark to see anything except the fore part of the engine. But as he straightened he heard the sound once more.

It was a voice—faint but unmistakable. It spoke a single word: "Ken!"

Sandy! Ken almost shouted his discovery aloud. With an enormous effort he restrained himself.

Sandy was back there, behind that protective timber

192

probably, in the very spot—! But how had it happened? Ken's thoughts were racing. Sandy must have fallen through the hatchway, right after he hauled Jackson off Ken's back. Was he hurt? Was he lying there helpless?

Ken gripped the ladder to prevent himself from diving through the opening. He must be more cautious than ever now, so that—

"Ken!" The voice was stronger this time, and closer.

"Shut up!" Anthony growled. "I'm trying to listen."

For an instant Ken froze. If Sandy called once more, and Anthony realized that he was on board—

"I will not shut up!" Ken said loudly. "I started to ask you when are we—?"

"What's the matter with you?" Anthony's head thrust downward toward him. "I said keep it quiet!"

"Why should I? Just because you've got a gun pointed at me?" Ken had twisted around to look up into Anthony's face, but he was speaking as distinctly as he could. "I know exactly what you're going to do. You're going to lock me in the cabin and then wreck the boat on the rocks!"

Anthony ripped the throttle wide open and the *Sea Robin* lurched forward. "Since you know so much," he called down, "you must know there's nothing you can do about it."

The noise of the engine filled his ears. Ken raised his voice: he had to let Sandy know just what the situation was, get a message to him before Anthony discovered his presence. "There's plenty I can do. I can rip the wires off the spark plugs. I can—"

Anthony's flashlight bore down, impaling Ken in a bright cone of light that made his slightest move evident from above. "Just try it. Go ahead—see if you can move faster than a bullet!"

"We've still got about five minutes before you jump overboard," Ken called back. "You won't be able to watch me every second. I'll figure something out!"

Anthony didn't answer. In scornful silence he manipulated the wheel, the gun still steady in his hand.

Ken could feel his nails biting into his palms. Had Sandy understood the information and the suggestion he had tried so desperately to get through to him? Or was he badly hurt, so that no matter how well he understood there was nothing he could do? If Sandy were helpless—

Ken leaned forward on the seat. He had to find out—get at least one look at Sandy to see if—

The engine coughed.

Instinctively Ken straightened. The flashlight dropped closer again, and with it the muzzle of the gun.

"What are you doing?" Anthony had bent down so that his head was only an arm's distance from Ken's shoulder.

Ken gathered his legs under him. If he jumped up suddenly, his shoulder would reach Anthony's jaw. The gun would go off, of course, but—

The engine coughed again, and then again. Ken waited, not moving, feeling Anthony's intent eyes on his rigid back.

The gun nudged him savagely. "Get up forward!" Anthony ordered.

The engine was missing badly now—only a few of its cylinders were firing properly. The *Sea Robin*, shuddering spasmodically, was rapidly losing its headway.

Ken moved slowly between the bunks, bracing himself on the rails as the boat rolled and wallowed.

"All the way!" Anthony said. "I don't know how you did it—but it isn't going to do you any good." He dropped down the last step and, still facing Ken, kneeled in front of the bulkhead opening. "Don't make a move," he cautioned. "Don't think I can't look at the engine and keep an eye on you too."

In another second, Ken knew, Anthony would turn his light through the opening. Where was Sandy?

"Look," Ken began desperately, fighting for time.

But even as he spoke, the realization came to him that in another moment it would be too late—they would be beyond help. Already the *Sea Robin* was surging forward on the great swells that raced the last half mile to shore, to crash thunderously on the rocks. A bit closer to shore and not even the engine could buck that irresistible pull.

"Shut up!" Anthony barked. His flash was already pivoting toward the opening. The aim of the gun was steady on Ken's stomach.

Ken's knees bent slightly, his weight coming forward. It was a short leap across the cabin—

"The wires are off!" There was blank amazement in Anthony's voice.

Then it happened! A sheet of white shot out of the hold!

It covered Anthony like a tent. In an instant he had disappeared from Ken's startled gaze, completely shrouded in the cloudlike fog that spread from the opening.

Ken took off—not in a headlong dive—in a feet-first

plunge, as if he were sliding for home plate in the last inning of a tie-score game.

He felt his toes strike something yielding. His back jarred heavily against the floor. Something hard thumped near by.

The white foam was spreading out widely into the cabin now, covering everything with a slippery slime. Ken got halfway up and slipped. He grabbed for a bunk and pulled himself erect.

There was vague movement under the thick layer of blanketing whiteness. Anthony was groping for the gun that had fallen from his hand when Ken had struck.

Ken thrust both arms elbow-deep into the bubbles. One hand clutched hair, the other cloth. Ken hauled Anthony up, first to his knees and then, by hoisting him against a bunk support, to his feet. Ken drew back his right arm then drove it forward once, twice, three times.

As Anthony's body slumped he hung onto it and lowered it to a bunk.

Ken gulped in a single breath of air, then let it out in a yell. "Sandy!"

Footsteps sounded on the deck, and a familiar shape loomed at the head of the ladder, dimly outlined against the night sky. "Here I am. You O.K.?"

"Are you?" Ken slid and stumbled across the cabin to meet him. His fingers found the light switch beside the door. For an instant they stared at each other, while behind Ken the foam on the floor billowed gently. More white suds were still pouring from the foam fire extinguisher now visible alongside the engine.

Sandy was all right!

But just as Ken realized it, he became aware of something else: above the creaking of the boat's timbers, through the silence of her dead engine, there was the sound of water crashing on rocks.

"Quick!" Ken yelled. "The engine—"

Sandy leaped down into the cabin and ducked toward the hold.

Ken waited only long enough to grab up Anthony's flashlight, still gleaming through its sticky coating, and then he was on deck. Frantically his fingers flipped every switch on the panel. The running lights blinked on, the searchlight cut a path through the darkness, lighting up the curving white manes of breakers dead ahead.

"Try it!" Sandy bellowed.

Ken jabbed the starter. The engine split, coughed, finally caught. The *Sea Robin* lifted and lurched ahead, aimed along the finger of light that showed white water and spray only a few hundred feet beyond the bow.

Ken threw out the clutch, jammed the lever into reverse, and let out the clutch again. The boat shuddered as the screw spun backward.

With what seemed infinite slowness the engine battled the momentum of the waves, pistons straining against their pull. Gradually—very gradually—the *Sea Robin* lost forward motion, shivered almost to a standstill, the power of the waves and the power of the engine deadlocked.

Finally one wave moved past—and then another and another. Inch by inch the *Sea Robin* fought for her life. Inch by inch she crept back from disaster. The swells were dashing over the low stern, flooding the deck with water—but no longer were they carrying the *Sea Robin* on with them toward the black rocks ahead.

Sandy struggled out on deck, past a wash of water tumbling into the cabin. He leaped to the hatchway and slammed its cover down. "Turn her!" he yelled.

Ken had already begun to pull the wheel carefully to port. Slowly the stern slewed around. He pulled harder.

The *Sea Robin* presented her broad flank to the swells—and the swells washed over her, bearing her relentlessly shoreward again.

Ken threw the clutch and shifted to forward speed. The bow came up. Ken thrust with all his strength on the wheel, forcing it around—farther, farther.

A huge wave came in from the front quarter, staggered the *Sea Robin*, drove her down. But she came up again.

Very slowly but steadily she nosed around toward the open sea. And then she was taking the swells full head on—riding over them, shaking herself free of their ponderous weight.

The engine was singing now, all its cylinders throbbing. At the *Sea Robin's* stern her wake flew high—like a gusty laugh tossed over her shoulder at the receding rocks.

With a single impulse the boys let out a triumphant yell. They were free! Before their voices died, the waves were quieter, the *Sea Robin's* speed smoothly quickening.

"Anthony!" Sandy said a moment later. "I'd better go take a look."

Ken turned him around. "Look at that first."

A mile out to sea a searchlight had come alive, its probing beam sweeping wide bright paths across the water. Ken turned their own lights so that it shone first to port and then to starboard and worked the switch on and off in a pattern of dots and dashes.

The other light answered and then flicked out. The red and green running lights came rapidly nearer. And between them it was soon possible to make out the low black shape of the *Dolphin,* riding fast and slicing through the water with the smoothness of a steel-edged blade.

Ken and Sandy grinned at each other.

"I always said the *Dolphin* was a mighty pretty little boat," Sandy said.

CHAPTER XXI

ALL CLEAR!

KEN AND SANDY had no idea, as they watched the *Dolphin* draw near, that their own excitement was being mirrored in a dozen other places at the same time. Orders were being barked into telephones and microphones, New York customs men were converging on certain particularly interesting localities—including Vic Samson's palatial apartment and the office of the Sea Food Restaurant Corporation—and other customs men were aboard a cutter heading out to quarantine to meet an incoming ship. They would have been interested in the news, but even without it they had enough to occupy their attention.

When the *Dolphin* was only a hundred feet away, her searchlight stabbed out, blinding them. "Kill your light!" It was an order, not a request.

Sandy flipped the switch and they stood waiting in the white glare.

"Jackson said you were aboard," a voice said. "But we didn't believe him." Jones stepped into the glow of a light on the bridge, the machine gun ready in his arm. "Where's Anthony?"

"Down below," Ken answered.

"Unconscious," Sandy added.

"Haul him on deck." The *Dolphin* edged up until a scant twenty-five feet separated the two boats. Jones's thin figure was a grim shape at the wheel. But his narrow face creased in a sudden grin when Anthony's limp form, still hung with wreaths of white foam, was deposited on the *Sea Robin's* deck. "What happened?" Jones asked then. "Looks like he fell in a washing machine."

Ken grinned back. "Fire extinguisher."

Jones sobered. "How'd he get aboard?"

"Jumped," Ken explained. "While you had your light off the *Stingray* for a minute."

"That was *after* you threw the others overboard— Jackson and Burns and—"

"Threw them overboard!" Sandy exploded. "They were all set to jump—as soon as they'd fixed the *Sea Robin* to ram you. We just"—Sandy's voice faltered briefly—"helped a little at the last minute."

Jones eyed them curiously and then, as if he had made up his mind, gestured toward Anthony. "Tie him up. I'd give you a pair of handcuffs, but there aren't any left." Once more he flashed his sudden grin. "Thompson's got our whole supply in use aboard the *Stingray.*"

When Anthony had been securely bound, hand and foot, Jones nodded his satisfaction. "Go ahead now," he said. "I'll follow you in."

Ken gulped. "We can't," he said. "We don't know anything about navigation."

Jones studied them for one more long moment before

he reached for his throttle. "All right," he said slowly. "You follow me. I'll take it easy."

The first rays of the sun came up over the ocean as they rounded the headland, and it was broad daylight before they took the *Sea Robin* carefully through the inlet and across the harbor toward the Batesons' dock where several figures stood waiting. When they finally edged up alongside the *Dolphin* and the *Stingray*, Jones came aboard to take over the controls. He was still eying them curiously, but there no longer seemed to be any real suspicion in his glance.

"O.K.," he said briskly, cutting the ropes around Anthony's ankles and hauling him to his feet. "We've got your friends waiting for you."

"You two all right?" It was Ted, calling from the dock.

"Sure," Ken called back, turning now to see the whole Bateson family, Thompson, Hank, and three strangers waiting for them to disembark.

Almost immediately two of the strangers stepped forward, took Anthony off Jones's hands, and whisked him up the dock and into a car that roared off up the driveway an instant later.

Ken's legs were shaky when he stepped off the *Sea Robin*, and Sandy too seemed to move more slowly than usual. There were a lot of voices all asking questions at once.

"Come on." It was Hank's laconic drawl that cut through them. "You all need to get right up to the house and have some coffee. We've got it waiting for you."

Ken had several swallows of the scalding liquid before he looked around at the crowded kitchen table, exchanged a tired grin with Sandy, and tried to concentrate on what was being said.

Thompson was speaking, his round face as genial as ever. "Anthony owned the Live Lobster then," he was saying, "and had been buying stolen lobsters from Jackson for quite a spell. But the restaurant didn't make money fast enough to suit him, so he got together with Vic Samson."

Ken cut in. "We caught on to that as soon as we heard that Samson owned the house Jackson lives in." He grinned and corrected himself. "*Lived* in, I mean."

Thompson turned his head to stare at the two boys. "You knew that? What made you investigate that?"

"A hunch," Ken answered. "There had to be some tie-up if the thing was to make any sense at all—especially after we got on the track of the marked plugs."

"Wait a minute!" Jones interjected. "What's this about marked plugs?"

"Didn't you know about the marked plugs?" Sandy asked. "That's how they got the smuggled diamonds into the restaurant."

"Smuggled diamonds!" Ted almost bounced to his feet. "What is all this about? I thought we were chasing lobster pirates."

Ken grinned at him. "That's what we thought, too, but it's only part of it." He turned to Thompson. "Why did they bother with the pirate business? I should think that would draw attention to their activities."

Thompson shook his head. "Seems as if we'll have to explain this thing together. We know some things you two don't, but you evidently know a lot of things we didn't tumble to. I'll fill in the background; you add the odd facts as they come up." He turned to his partner. "You'd better take some notes—we'll need them for our report."

Jones fished in his pocket for a pencil and a note-book. "Matter of fact," he said to Thompson, "I'm not sure we'd have a report without the things these boys seem to have discovered."

Thompson nodded. "You've got something there." He lighted a cigarette before he started. "Smuggling's a mighty tough business. Smugglers have to bring in a lot of stuff to make it pay, and they can't expect to get away with big-scale operations for very long because the customs men of all countries work pretty close together. On this case, for example, we got our first tip from reputable gem importers on this side of the ocean. They said there seemed to be a lot of diamonds floating around—more than could be accounted for by legiti-mate imports. We checked the diamond centers in Europe and found that there were several well-known smugglers making trips to this country, and that their friends were active in the diamond market. We watched the men closely and searched them and their luggage carefully each time they entered. We even sent opera-tives to make the crossing with them." He grinned ruefully. "Couldn't find a thing."

"Trouble was," Jones took it up as Thompson reached for his coffee cup, "we didn't think it possible for the courier to get rid of the stones five or six miles offshore. Diamonds are too valuable to throw overboard in the hope that your man'll pick them up. You have to be sure they'll be found. Our man made four trips across before he got his first lead. He found that they always used a boat that skirted Long Island on its way in, and that they always booked a stateroom on the starboard side —the side facing the shore when the boat passed the island. On the fifth trip our man had a cabin right next to our suspect—and that time he caught a signal— blinking lights from a boat."

Sandy cut in. "When the liner reached a certain spot —in line with two buoys—Jackson's boat, already on the spot, flashed the signal. The man on the liner flashed back and then threw the tube overboard."

"Tube?" Mr. Bateson asked. "What tube?"

"That part of it," Thompson said to Ken, "you know better than we do. You take it for a while."

"The diamonds," Ken said, "were packed in an aluminum tube. It had a radio transmitter inside and a small bell outside. Jackson or Anthony could find the tube in the dark by using a radio direction finder. That got them pretty close and they did the rest of the job by listening for the sound of the small bell."

"But it all sounds so elaborate—so complicated." Mrs. Bateson looked at them wonderingly over the coffeepot.

"Worth it, though," Thompson assured her. "There was about a quarter of a million dollars worth of stones in that tube tonight." He looked at Ken. "We didn't know about the tube until we caught Anthony out there. We knew about the signal, as I said, and that gave us the general locality out here, but we had trouble going on from there. Neither Anthony nor Samson—we knew about their being connected through the restaurant— had ever been involved in smuggling before. We checked them, but we couldn't turn anything up. We checked Anthony extra thoroughly because it seemed strange to us that he should suddenly become a lobster-man. It didn't occur to us for quite a while to worry about Jackson because we thought he was nothing more than a small-time lobster pirate—which was exactly what Anthony wanted us to think."

"Of course," Jones said with a smile, "if we'd thought of checking the ownership of the house Jackson lives in, as you two did, we could have gotten ahead much faster."

"Anthony's a cool customer," Thompson continued. "Even when he knew we were keeping an eye on him he kept his head."

"You shouldn't have done your fisherman routine with only twenty feet of line on your rod," Sandy said, grinning. He was looking almost himself again except for the swelling lump on his head where he had struck the hatchway when he tumbled back through it.

"You were following Anthony that night," Ken said, "weren't you? The night we were all out trying to catch Jackson?"

Thompson nodded. "Anthony led us neatly out of the way so that Jackson, with his handy underwater exhaust, could make the pickup as usual. But we began to realize what was going on, and when you boys talked about that long-distance shot of the *Sea Robin* we got pretty excited, especially since Anthony was being so helpful about developing it." Thompson shook his head regretfully. "I thought he might do something to ruin the negative and I tried to warn you, but—"

"The film came out all right," Sandy said calmly. He went on to tell them how he had managed to circumvent the spoiled developer. "It shows Jackson and Plauk and one of the cylinders," he concluded.

"We're having better luck than we deserve," Jones said to Thompson. "Maybe we ought to resign and let Ken and Sandy take over our jobs," he added, smiling.

"We weren't so bright," Sandy said hastily, wary as usual of being praised. "We still don't know why Jackson had to be brought into the plot. Why couldn't Anthony have made his own pickups?"

"Because people expected him to be out at night— while they'd be suspicious if Anthony took to leaving after dark." Jones looked up from his notebook. "Now what about those marked plugs?"

Ken told them about how the marked plugs were used to denote the diamond-loaded claws while the Batesons listened openmouthed and Thompson and Jones nodded approvingly.

"And I told you they didn't amount to anything." Ted shook his head sadly. "I'd better stick to fishing, I guess."

"Maybe we'd better too," Sandy added. "We sure missed our chance at the restaurant tonight."

Thompson sighed. "You were there too? When?"

Sandy told them of the chase in the building. "I guess Samson's got a headache now," he finished. "Anyway, he ought to have. We hit him hard enough."

"He's got a bigger headache than that coming up," Jones said. "He's got a long spell ahead of him as a guest of Uncle Sam."

"I was at the restaurant too," Thompson put in. "But I didn't get even as close to anything as you did." He looked at Ken from beneath lowered eyebrows. "I suppose you know I was run off the road."

Ken nodded. "We didn't stop because we were sure you were part of another gang," he admitted. "How'd you get out here ahead of us?" he added hastily.

Thompson grinned. "I'm happy to hear there's something about this case you don't know. We went across the road to LaGuardia Field and got a Coast Guard plane to run us out here."

"Why didn't you raid the Live Lobster?" Sandy asked.

"Because we couldn't be sure the diamonds were sent there. We checked up every lobster Jackson sold the day after you took that picture, but you know none of *his* lobsters held anything. That's the really smart part of their plan. Anthony couldn't be suspected because he didn't go out at night, and Jackson never held on to the diamonds longer than it took to put them in lobsters with marked claws and dump the lobsters into one of Anthony's traps."

"So that's why we sometimes found our traps untouched even when we knew Jackson had been out at night," Ted muttered. "When he was picking up diamonds he was too busy to steal lobsters."

"Well," Ken said after a pause, "let's—"

"Hold up a minute." Thompson pinned Ken with a glance. "At first I thought it was just a stupid move on Anthony's part, but after hearing all you did in this case, I think you had something to do with it."

"With what?" Sandy asked.

"With getting Anthony to lead us right to the point of picking up the cylinder tonight," Thompson said. "Why did he do that?"

"We have to plead guilty," Ken said. "We heard Anthony give Burns his instructions, and we figured we could give him the signal and make him lead you right to the spot."

"That's what I call smart thinking," Mr. Bateson said.

Jones nodded. "It closed the case for us." He put away the notebook. "I suppose that's—"

"Wait a moment." Thompson still sounded unsatisfied. He turned to Ken. "You two are much too smart to stick your necks in a noose. What made you stow away on the *Sea Robin?*"

"For a little excitement," Sandy said quickly.

Thompson shook his head. "That's not the way you boys operate—you seem to have a good reason for everything you do."

There was a moment of silence before Ken spoke. "We realized we'd done a stupid thing—putting you out there with two boats against you." He shrugged. "So we—"

"So you went along for the ride and saved our lives," Thompson concluded. "They *were* going to ram us, weren't they?"

"You'd have been all right, anyway," Sandy said.

"You don't think they'd have picked us up even if we survived the crash, do you?" Jones asked.

"Look," Sandy cut in. "Never mind that. Tell us what they did if fog or something else made it impossible for them to throw the cylinder overboard." His face was a fiery red.

Jones changed the subject for Sandy's sake. "In that case the stones would go right back to Europe—the courier always booked a return trip to forestall that kind of emergency. They'd try it again right away. At least that's what we figure."

Thompson nodded. "That's what Jackson said on the way in." He looked at Jones. "Let's get this stuff to headquarters and see what the boys got out of Samson and his crowd at the restaurant." He spoke to the boys. "You'll have to sign some affidavits." He smiled at Sandy. "And your modesty won't get you out of a thing."

Sandy leaped up, knocking his chair over behind him. "We haven't called Global yet! Come on, Ken! Why, this story will—"

"This story will be given to all the papers and wire services at the same time," Thompson said firmly.

Ken was on his feet too. What, he wondered, would a top newspaperman like his father do in a spot like this? Would he stand by and let Global get its story at the same time everybody else did?

"Wouldn't you like a print of that picture Sandy took?" he heard himself asking.

"Yes, of course," Thompson said. "We'll need it for—"

"Well"—Ken grinned—"we want to call Global."

For a moment their eyes met, and then the round genial face crinkled into a grin. "I don't have any control over what you do after we leave," Thompson said finally. "And we're leaving the minute we get that print."

Sandy went outside with them to hand the print over, but he paused a moment on the way to whisper to Ken. "When you call Granger tell him he'll find the negative under the enlarger easel."

Ken grinned at his back and when he turned around

he found the Batesons' expressions mirroring his own.

"What I say," Hank announced suddenly, "is that we let Ken and Sandy get some sleep, while we round up the Eastend lobstermen for a party tonight. Sort of a celebration."

"That's the longest speech I ever heard you make, Hank," Mrs. Bateson said admiringly. "And it's also a wonderful idea."

"Sure is," Ted agreed. "Remember, Dad," he went on, turning to his father, "how you were afraid Ken and Sandy might get into trouble if they stayed here?"

The wrinkles in the fisherman's weather-beaten face deepened. "Well, looks like I was right," he said mildly. "They did." Then he added soberly, "But I guess I don't have to tell you how much we appreciate—"

"We never mean to get into trouble," Ken interrupted him, edging toward the door.

Sandy returned in time to hear his friend's statement. "That's right," he agreed. "We don't mean to. But somehow we manage it pretty often just the same."

Sandy was right. And when, a few weeks later, they innocently stopped their red convertible to offer a ride to a weary hitchhiker, they were again—without meaning to—letting themselves in for the trouble that came to be known as *The Secret of the Coiled Cobra*.

he found his appeal

left at and made up

the casual freshman for a pair of a
celebration.

"That's not bad, myself, I ever cheer you make,"
Huck, like Harrison and admiringly. "And it's also a
well laid scheme."

"Sure it," Tel smiled. "Remember," he went on,
turning to his father, "how you were afraid Ken and
Sandy might get too much if they stayed here?"

The writer asked the odd man's weather rather face
deepened. "Well, looks that way, right," he said coldly.
"They did," Tom he said decidedly. "But I guess I don't
have to tell you how much we appreciate—"

"We must mean to get into trouble," Ken interrupted
him, edging toward the door.

Sandy returned in time to his friend's statement.
"That's right," he agreed. "We don't want to. But somehow we manage to get in their hair the same."

Sandy watched Ken when a few weeks later they
innocently stopped Harrison managed to unload the
non-appointed as they went again—without meaning to. During that, I realize the families that came
to bide—some of the rest of their behind it obeying.